Highways of
the Heart

Books by George H. Morrison

Highways of the Heart

Wind on the Heath

Highways of
the Heart

George H. Morrison

kregel
PUBLICATIONS

Grand Rapids, MI 49501

Highways of the Heart by George H. Morrison.

Copyright © 1994 by Kregel Publications.

Published in 1994 by Kregel Publications, a division of Kregel, Inc., P.O. Box 2607, Grand Rapids, MI 49501. Kregel Publications provides trusted, biblical publications for Christian growth and service. Your comments and suggestions are valued.

Cover Photograph: POSITIVE IMAGES, Patricia Sgrignoli
Cover and Book Design: Alan G. Hartman

Library of Congress Cataloging-in-Publication Data
Morrison, George H. (George Herbert), 1866-1928.
  Highways of the heart: 60 sermons that touch the heart / George H. Morrison.
      p.   cm. (The Morrison Classic Sermon Series)
  Originally published: London: Hodder and Stoughton, 1926.
    1. Sermons, English—Scotland. 2. United Free Church of Scotland—Sermons. 3. Presbyterian Church—Scotland—Sermons. I. Title. II. Series: Morrison, George H. (George Herbert). The Morrison Classic Sermon Series.
BX9178.M6H54   1993   252'.052—dc20   93-37827
                                             CIP
  ISBN 0-8254-3290-1 (paperback)

            1 2 3 4 5 Printing / Year 98 97 96 95 94

Printed in the United States of America

Contents

Publisher's Foreword

One wonders if the old wit's comment on sermons applies to sermon books as well when he said that a sermon was something a preacher would travel across the country to give but most people wouldn't walk across the street to hear. The initial response to a book of sermons by a turn-of-the-century Scotsman may be somewhat skeptical—in an era dominated by sophisticated media, savvy marketing analysis, and seeker-sensitive communication models, the pressured pastor might wonder about the benefits of reading "relic" sermons.

It was C.S. Lewis who referred to the historical fallacy of regarding works of the past, particularly the classics and the Bible, as irrelevant and untrustworthy based on the criterion of age alone. His comment—"This mistaken preference for the modern books and this shyness of the old ones is nowhere more rampant than in theology."—applies equally as well to pastoral theology.[1]

Issues of truth ought not to be subject to a statute of limitations, but to paraphrase Thomas Oden, we blithely assume that in preaching—"just as in corn poppers, electric toothbrushes, and

---

1. C.S. Lewis, "On the Reading of Old Books" in God in the Dock, ed. Walter Hooper (Grand Rapids: Eerdmans, 1970), 200.

automobile exhaust systems—new is good, newer is better, and newest is best."[2] Morrison's sermons represent, without question, not only a different culture (early twentieth-century Scotland which had more in common with the nineteenth century than with our own era) but also a different pastoral model. If pastors are physicians of the soul, then Morrison's ministry had more in common with the hometown doctor who made housecalls (Morrison was legendary for his visitation ministry, sometimes averaging 1000 calls a year) than the modern medical specialist (and pastor) with his sophisticated array of technology.

Morrison's value, therefore, for the modern pastor-preacher does not lie in his insights into church management, church growth, or contemporary worship. Morrison most likely would have eschewed the whole notion of a "contemporary gospel." What he would have championed today—passionately and patiently—was the relevant and compelling presentation of biblical truth that touches both the intellects and the emotions of contemporary listeners. His value for the modern reader lies in appreciating and learning from a style and sermonic approach that was contemporary in its time and whose principles have enduring value.

What can we learn, then, from Morrison? For one thing, he respected the intelligence of his listeners. His sermons are filled with allusions and quotations from a wide range of literature common to the experience of his people—Burns, Milton, Dickens, and Shakespeare—but without any hint of intellectualism or pedantry. Morrison perfectly prefigures Charles Swindoll's comment that preachers should get a good education and then get over it!

Modern preachers would do well to analyze Morrison's style of literary reference and determine the common cultural mediums of our own day. Lacking a similarly cohesive cultural identity, we may have to search harder for the insightful reference or provide a window for the congregation through which to view another world (consider, for example, the difference between quoting Shakespeare and any current TV commercial). Morrison not only spoke of beautiful truths, but he sought to speak the truth beautifully and for help turned to the great English writers and poets.

---

2. Thomas Oden, "On Not Whoring After the Spirit of the Age," in *No God But God*, ed. Os Guinness and John Seel (Chicago: Moody Press, 1992), 195.

Morrison also placed the sermon in a strategic context—the awful carnage of World War I (where Morrison's own son was killed), the emerging discoveries of modern science, or the urbanization of the once predominately rural Scottish society and the corresponding problems of secularization, alienation, and loneliness. Morrison addressed the developing cultural, social, and political dynamics of the day with both challenging and comforting truths from the Word. If we look closely at the changing demographics and family structures in our own society, we will find ample opportunities for strategically-formulated points of reference.

One other obvious characteristic of Morrison's sermons are their personal appeal. Morrison spoke directly to the needs and concerns of real people: the grieving, the lonely, the guilt-ridden, the worried, and the spiritually hungry. He described his approach as, "It has been my habit. . . at the evening service to allow myself a wider scope. . . to win the attention, in honorable ways, of some at least of that vast class of people who today sit so lightly to the church." Judging from the full pews at the Wellington United Free Church, the success of his sermons can be measured by the phrase used in Mark 12:37—"The common people heard him gladly."

In this new edition of Morrison's sermons, Kregel Publications has attempted to "open a window" into the culture of Morrison's ministry and times. Uncommon terms (in today's usage) have been noted, and the frequent quotes, allusions, and personalities identified. In a few places grammatical constructions that might have rolled off the Scottish tongue have been modified with the modern reader in mind. It is our hope that by appreciating the richness of Morrison's style, readers will be encouraged to creatively speak to both the intellect and emotion of today's congregations. Lewis's comments are a fitting encouragement: "Every age has its own outlook. It is especially good at seeing certain truths and specially liable to make certain mistakes. We all, therefore, need the books that will correct the characteristic mistakes of our own period. And that means old books."[3]

DENNIS R. HILLMAN, Senior Editor

---

3. Lewis, 202.

Introduction

Dr. George Herbert Morrison has a gift of saying things that we all would have said, had it occurred to us to say them; and he said those inevitable things as we could not, in English prose that had the effect of "poetry on the heart." This quotation of James Denney aptly sums up the "secret"—if there was such a thing—of Dr. Morrison's classic sermons delivered from his pulpit in Wellington Church, Glasgow, Scotland, from 1902 to 1928.

Throughout his ministry he was known for his concentrated study, his regular pastoral visitation, and his constant writing for publication. His appeal lay not in any physical stature, for he lacked that; not in any tricks or oratory, for he never preached for effect; but in the quiet winsome way in which he spoke to the heart from a heart suffused with the love and grace of Christ. He never lost sight of the fact that as a minister of Christ his first concern must be how best to bring his hearers closer to the heart of the Lord.

Although written early in this century, his sermons are modern in touch and spirit; the tone and temper are admirably effective for use today. Their simplicity of phrase came out of arduous toil as the writer worked in his preparation. The style is the man—quiet and genial—and his preaching was like this. Morrison was always the pastor preacher, ever seeking to meet life's needs with some word from God.

Whatever he did had the hallmark of preparation and finality. Some sermons came easily like the bird on the wing; others came after much hard work and sweat of mind and heart. The fact that he brooded over his texts with something of an artist's unconsciousness and superb leisure is one of the elements in his power as a preacher. He brooded over the Word of God until it became translucent. His loyalty to Christ and his devotion in the secret place are wedded to his daily practice of study and writing.

His counsel to the young preacher is most revealing as the secret of his own success: "I can think of nothing, except that young preachers will do well to guard against the tendency to rush which is the bane of modern life. The habit of unprofitable bustle and rush, the present-day preoccupation with small affairs and engagements, is withholding many good things from us. For myself it is essential that I have leisure to brood and meditate."

To read and study these selections from the author's many volumes of messages will be to open new vistas of truth and to learn how old and familiar truths can be clothed in fresh and living words which will glow with unsuspected meaning.

RALPH G. TURNBULL

Biographical Sketch

It used to be said that just as visitors to London in bygone days felt that they must of necessity hear Spurgeon or Parker or Liddon, so visitors to Glasgow in more recent years had the feeling that they could not miss hearing Dr. George H. Morrison in Wellington Church. One of the most noted of English Bishops, after fulfilling an afternoon engagement at the University, hurried off to be in time for the evening service at Wellington. And the miner from Fifeshire or the crofter[1] from the Hebrides, spending a Sunday in Glasgow, would have considered the day incomplete if he did not hear Dr. Morrison.

To Glasgow Dr. Morrison's ministry at Wellington was something like what Dr. Alexander Whyte's ministry at St. George's was to Edinburgh. Different in many ways, they were alike in the extent to which they captured the community and maintained their unbroken hold year after year.

Dr. Morrison was a great preacher who was also a great pastor. Of this rather unusual combination he was, indeed, the supreme example.

His genius as a preacher was never more clearly shown than by his success in solving the problem of the second service. Shortly after his settlement in Glasgow, the afternoon service was giving

---

1. a tenant farmer

13

place to an evening one, but the results in general were not too satisfactory. When Wellington decided on an evening service Dr. Morrison was determined to give it a distinctive character. In the mornings he adhered to the old Scottish tradition of expository preaching.

In the evenings he allowed himself a wider scope, presenting the Christian essentials in a somewhat different setting and, as he said, calling to his help every type of illustrative aid that appealed to him. He strove to give these evening addresses a strong human interest in order, as he put it, "to win the attention, in honorable ways, of some at least of the vast class of people who sit very loosely to the Church. The touch is naturally far lighter than in the morning, but this does not mean lack of preparation. I prepare as carefully for the one as for the other." His one aim in preaching, he once said, was "to help people along the road." Here I may interpolate how Dr. Morrison once told me that, after he had fully prepared his subject, he set himself the task of striving to see how simply he could present it. His simplicity, therefore, was not the easy, facile thing some may have supposed it to be; it was the fruit of definite and earnest effort.

The response at his evening service was immediate and striking. The church became crowded to overflowing; long queues formed in University Avenue before the doors were opened and this was no mere passing phase. The same state of matters continued for over twenty-six years, right to the end of his ministry. And he got the class of people he set out to reach. These crowded evening congregations at Wellington made an interesting study in themselves. All classes and all ages were represented, but young men and women were always largely in evidence. Nor were they there because of the prospect of any novelty or sensation. They could only have been drawn because they felt that their wistful longings and inarticulate yearnings were somehow met and answered by the man in the pulpit with the soft voice, the quiet effortless style, and the subtle elusive charm.

There was no clangorous or challenging presentation of a new Evangel. Dr. Morrison's secret was in taking old familiar truths and clothing them in fresh robes of language which made them sparkle with a luster of their own and revealed meanings hitherto hidden and unsuspected. He had a perfect flair in the selection of texts often fresh and suggestive. "He gave them drink out of the depths," "In the day that thou stoodest on the other side," "The deep that croucheth beneath," "Thou didst cleave the earth with rivers," are some that may be quoted, almost at random.

Many of his sermons were prose poems; all of them were suffused with a tender charm and rich in spiritual helpfulness. Volume after volume was published, and G. H. Morrison's sermons found a place in manse libraries everywhere, almost like those of F. W. Robertson of Brighton, while they also very markedly appealed to a wide circle of lay readers. They revealed him to be both a mystic and a man of letters and were acknowledged to place him in the foremost ranks of British preachers. . . .

There are many people who still remember this or that sermon of Dr. Morrison's; there are as many who love to recall instances of his pastoral devotion. His routine visitation, so extensive and incessant, was but one feature of his pastoral activity. Many tales could be told of his constant solicitous care of the sick and those in sorrow or trouble. And no success or joy that came to any member of any family in his congregation was overlooked or allowed to pass without letters or postcards from him which are still prized possessions.

The end of this notable ministry came swiftly and unexpectedly when Dr. Morrison was at the age of sixty-two, and while there was no sign of any waning of his powers and no abatement of his popularity. In the first week of October, 1928, he was back from his summer holiday—he held that a good holiday was a *sine qua non*[2] for a minister—and he was getting into the full stream of another winter's activities. On the Wednesday afternoon he had spent three continuous hours in the homes of his people, and in the evening he gave a memorable address to a small company of workers in the hall of Gorbals Church. On Thursday evening he became seriously ill, and on Sunday morning shortly after midnight he passed away almost before his illness had become generally known.

On the day before he died, when there was a slight rally, he was able to have in his hands one of the early copies of a book to which he had been looking forward—his biography, which I had written at the request of London publishers, and in the preparation of which he had given me every facility with his characteristic kindness.

---

2. something essential

Although Dr. Morrison did not reach the allotted span, he, if any man, had done what he used to call "a good day's darg."[3] He warned young preachers against unprofitable bustle and rush, and preoccupation with small affairs and trifling engagements. A master of method, he so ordered his time that, while he was never idle, he was never hurried or flurried. There was always about him a calm serenity, and as he moved among men he seemed a living epistle of what he preached.

Reprinted from Alexander Gammie, *Preachers I Have Heard*, Pickering & Inglis, Ltd. (London, n.d.)

Dedication

To the Misses Harvie

The friends of every good cause and my loyal helpers through many long years

---

3. a good day's work

"Ye have not passed this way heretofore"
(Joshua 3:4).

1

The Untrodden Way

There are some things we never get accustomed to, no matter how often they may be repeated. They thrill us every time that they arrive. No minister, however long his ministry, ever gets accustomed to a death-bed. Nobody, however hard his life is, ever gets accustomed to the spring. And always, right to the end of life, when the New Year comes stepping up to greet us, it evokes a certain response within the heart. It is true we do not measure life by years. We live in deeds, not breaths. Our reckonings are independent of the calendar. They are regulated by personal experiences. Yet is there something in a common pressure that adds to individual intensity, and that is always so at the New Year. We are like Israel on the banks of Jordan. We have reached an end which is also a beginning. As back of us all there is a common journey, so before us is an untrodden way. What, then, does this old story give us, to hearten and to guide us, as our feet cross the threshold of the year?

The first thing it impresses on us is that for the untrodden way *we must sanctify ourselves.* "Sanctify yourselves," said Joshua to the people, "for tomorrow the Lord will work wonders among you" (Joshua 3:5). You will note that when Israel reached Jordan they were not immediately ordered to its crossing. For three days they

lay upon its banks. They were remembering all the way the Lord
had led them. And then enriched by memory and mindful of a love
that never failed them, they were commanded to sanctify themselves. What that meant for *them* is a matter for scholars to determine. One turns to Exodus and to Leviticus to discover what that
meant for them. What that means for *us*, as we look forward to
another year, is to be gathered from the words of Jesus, "For their
sakes I sanctify Myself" (John 17:19). Facing the untrodden way,
we are to dedicate ourselves again to God. We are to give ourselves
to the duties of our calling with a fresh and unreserved surrender no
matter what our calling is, whether preaching the everlasting gospel
or glorifying His name upon a sick-bed. The wonders of tomorrow
depend on the sanctification of today. A new surrender here and
now is the prelude to a wonderful experience. All which ought to be
borne in mind by those who are growing weary of their work and
dreading the prospect of another year. The enthusiasm of youth
may have departed, the strength we once enjoyed may have been
weakened, the freshness may have been rubbed off things a little
through the ceaseless handling of the years; but if here and now
facing the unknown in our Lord's fashion we sanctify ourselves,
tomorrow shall be more wonderful than yesterday.

Another thing the story teaches is that for the untrodden way *we
need new commands*. This chapter, as one of the Puritans has said, is
notably a chapter of commands. There were long periods in the desert
journey when no new commands were given to Israel. They struck
their tents, they marched, they pitched again under the kindly leadership of Heaven. But now, facing the unknown way, there is more
than a general and kindly leadership, there are new commands for
every emergency. Arise—go forward—sanctify yourselves—take up—
pass over—come not near. Orders follow in a swift succession for
every step on that untrodden road from which I gather that, facing a
New Year, we can never rest on the commands of yesterday. We
want to be in living touch with God. That is why prayer is absolutely
necessary if the New Year is to be one of victory. Prayer keeps us in
living touch with Him who sees the end from the beginning. And if I
speak to any whose prayer-life has grown poor under the pressure of
multitudinous duties, may I beg of them to alter all that *now*. No
labor can take the place of prayer. No learning can take the place of
prayer. We are the followers of One who prayed and praying won

His triumph. In living, daily, personal touch with God there is strength as there is joy and peace for the darkest mile of the untrodden way.

I close by noting that for the untrodden way Israel *sent on ahead the Ark of God.* It was the sign and symbol that the Lord was with them, and they sent it on ahead into the swollen river. In spite of the express command of Jesus, how we send our imaginings ahead! How we toss ourselves into a fever over the fears of the untrodden way! But a living faith sends on the Ark of God, entrusts every tomorrow to His keeping, and when the floods come they do not overwhelm us. Fear is a poor hand at finding a place to wade across. Fear is a sorry bridge-builder. Fear drowns the music of today. It hears nothing but the rushing of the river. But Israel sent on the Ark of God, and that made all the difference for them as it makes all the difference for us. With a fresh surrender of ourselves, with a spirit receptive and responsive, with a profound conviction that God is on ahead ordering everything in perfect love, let us go forward with the banners flying to the high adventure of another year, for we have not passed this way heretofore.

"The stone which the builders refused is become the head stone of the corner. This is the Lord's doing; it is marvelous in our eyes" (Ps. 118:22–23).

2

The Ignorance of the Expert

Had it been others who had acted so, there would have been no occasion for surprise. The man in the street can scarcely be expected to be an authority on stones. If my watch gets out of order I should never dream of taking it to the shoemaker. If I did and if he made a mess of it, I should only have myself to blame. I naturally take it to the watchmaker who has been studying watches since first he was apprenticed and who in this particular business is an expert. The notable thing is that these builders were all experts. Stones were (if I might put it so) their bread. Daily they handled nothing else but stones. They were supposed to know everything about them. And yet these experts—these carefully trained specialists— had the witness of their folly facing them every time they passed the finished Temple. There, high up in the chief place of honor, was a stone they had condemned as useless. It was not hidden deep in the foundations. It was exalted so that every eye could see it. Someone had come along and had detected what none of the trained specialists had found—and the stone was now the headstone of the corner. Thus do we light on the important fact that specialists can be very

blind occasionally. Experts who give their nights and days to things may sometimes miss the thing that matters most. All which to dull, unlearned folk is often so exceedingly astonishing that they can only say, "This is the Lord's doing; it is marvelous in our eyes."
That ignorance of the expert is one of the common facts of life. And one says this without in the least disparaging all the magnificent service of the specialist. I think it is the Sadhu Sundar Singh[1] who tells of an Indian friend of his who was an expert botanist. He could tell you all about the daffodil and give you an exact description of it. Yet when daffodils were brought him as a gift once, he entirely failed to recognize them. He had never seen them growing in their beauty. That man was an accomplished botanist; he was an expert in his chosen science; he had mastered the orders and the genera and was an authority on habitats. Yet of the one thing that really matters in the daffodil, touching our wintry spirits to fine issues, he was more ignorant than any English girl. So men may know the planetary movements and never have felt the wonder of the stars. They may have mastered all the laws of rhythm, yet never been haunted by the spell of poetry. They may have studied Shakespeare with such assiduous care that they can tell you if a play is late or early, yet *Shakespeare* they may never have known. I am not disparaging the expert any more than I would the grammarian or Browning.[2] Advancing knowledge always needs the specialist, and our indebtedness to him is boundless. I only wish to suggest that not infrequently the expert loses the forest in the trees and somehow misses all that really matters.

I venture to think that, with peculiar force, this applies to the study of the Bible. Sometimes those who know most about the Bible know least of the living power of the book. It would be impossible to put in words our debt to the exact study of the Bible. To multitudes it is a new book altogether as the result of a sane and sober criticism. Yet there are times when one profoundly feels how a man may be an expert in the Scriptures and yet miss the only things that really matter. One may discuss the problem of the *Pentateuch* and do it with all the learning of the specialist; one may have mastered all that can be known of the relations of the *Synoptic*

1. Sadhu Sundar Singh (1889–1929), Indian missionary.
2. Robert Browning (1812–1889), English poet.

Gospels, and yet the *Bible*, the living word of God in its convicting and transforming power, may remain unto his heart as a sealed book.

Sometimes there is an ignorance in experts far deeper than the ignorance of common folk. They are like the Sadhu's Indian botanist who failed to recognize the daffodil. And all the time the poet and the child, ignorant of the elements of botany, may be enthralled and conquered by its loveliness. There is something more needed by the Bible than any exactitude of knowledge. The Bible only yields its inmost secret when deep begins calling unto deep. That is why some poor unlettered woman may have a far truer grasp of what the Bible is than the specialist who is versed in all its problems. It has found her and made her glad. To her it is a word to rest on. It has proved itself a light unto her path. It never fails her in any hour of need. And all this is so wonderful to her that like the Psalmist she can only say, "This is the Lord's doing; it is marvelous in our eyes."

We see the same fact with fullest clearness when we recall how Jesus was rejected. He came unto His own, says John, and His own received Him not. Now had the common folk alone rejected Him, we could scarcely have wondered at their doing so. For the common folk were looking for a king, and Jesus was not their idea of a king. The strange thing is that Jesus was rejected not by the common folk but by the Pharisees—and the Pharisees were Messianic experts. They were specialists in the doctrine of Messiah. They were reckoned to know everything about Him. Night and day they had studied the Old Testament with a zeal that was little short of heroism. Yet when Messiah came they failed to recognize Him though they had given many a learned lecture on Him just as the Sadhu's learned Indian friend failed to recognize the daffodil. The stone was not rejected by the passers-by. The stone was rejected by the *builders*—by the experts, the specialists in stones, the men who were held to know everything about them. When our Lord selected that great saying and deliberately applied it to Himself (Mark 12:10), was He not sounding a warning down the ages that sometimes the experts may be wrong?

"My peace I give unto you" (John 14:27).

3
Peace, the Possession of Adequate Resources

Talking with a young fellow some time ago, I was struck by a remark he made. It followed on a sermon which we both had listened to on the subject of interior peace. "It's not peace," he said, "we young fellows want. What we want is *thrills*." That was a very candid utterance, and one likes young fellows to be candid. It set me wondering whether inward peace was really so gray as it is sometimes painted. And just then in the book of an honored friend I lit on a sentence which arrested me. He said *peace is the possession of adequate resources*. That seemed to me a very fruitful thought with a strong appeal in it for vigorous minds, and it is well worth considering a little.

Think, for instance, how true that is of business. When long seasons of depression come, and when business is stagnant if not moribund, what is it that makes all the difference between intense anxiety and peace? It seems to me, who am not a business man but one who watches things with an observant eye, that it is just the possession of adequate resources. If there be little capital and almost no reserves, how terrible these dead times must be! I sometimes wonder how a business man can sleep not knowing if he can tide it over. But how different when these dead seasons come for any business that has great reserves and is strong in the possession of vast capital. Scanty capital means sleepless hours. Inadequate resources spell anxiety. What fears and miseries must haunt the breast when there is almost nothing to fall back upon! I venture to think that in the realm of business when times are bad and everything is stagnant, peace is the possession of adequate resources.

The same thing is true of higher spheres. Think, for example, of creative genius. Contrast the toiling literary hack[1] with the man of genius like Sir Walter Scott.[2] The one, very imperfectly endowed, is always in misery lest he be running dry. I have known preachers who were just like that—haunted by the fear of running dry. But the man of genius is serene and confident as Sir Walter was serene and confident because conscious of perfectly adequate resources. "Here is God's plenty," as Dryden[3] said of Chaucer.[4] I have known three or four great men in my life, and there was one feature common to them all. They never worried and they rarely hurried. There was a leisurely serenity about them. And that peace whatever their task might be, whether laying the Atlantic cable or building the Forth bridge, was the possession of adequate resources, not in the bank but in the brain.

Then one turns to our Lord and at once discovers how true that was of Him. It was one of the secrets of His so rich serenity. Look at Him in the storm—how calm He is! Look again—He is lying fast asleep. He is peaceful amid the raging elements, slumbering like an infant in its cradle. And all the others, Peter, James, and John, are agitated, excited, and alarmed, fearful amid the terrors of the sea. *Their* fear betrayed their helplessness. It showed them unequal to their problem. They were not equipped for battling with storms. They had no reserves to call up for a tempest. But He was peaceful and sleeping like a child though the wind was howling and the boat was filling, and His peace was the possession of adequate resources. Picture the anxious look upon the host's face when the wine gave out at the marriage-feast at Cana (John 2:3). Even Mary was distressed about it, worrying over the honor of the

---

1. an uninspired writer
2. Sir Walter Scott (1771–1832), Scottish novelist and poet.
3. John Dryden (1631–1700), English poet, dramatist and critic.
4. Geoffrey Chaucer (1340?–1400), English poet.

family. Christ alone was care-free. Christ alone was radiant and serene because conscious of perfectly adequate resources. "My peace"—it was a very wonderful peace. No sounding of our thought can ever fathom it. There was perfect fellowship with God in it. There was full and unconditional surrender. But one element, one vital element, witnessed in a score of incidents was the possession of adequate resources.

Then the Master comes to you and says, "My peace I give unto you." And perhaps, like my young friend you say, "I do not want that peace. I want to have a vivid, thrilling time of it." Many people are saying that today. Well, now, think of it like this—lay aside the unwelcome sense of peace as if peace meant taking the color out of life and robbing experience of its vividness. Instead of that, say to yourself quietly and say it again and again until you have mastered it: *peace is the possession of adequate resources.* You want to live a full, abundant life; but are you really equipped for such a life? Is your will strong enough—your feeling fine enough—your conscience quiet enough—your heart deep enough? Then Christ comes and says, "Friend, enter into My fellowship today, and I shall give you the resources that you need." Christ can take the sting out of the conscience. Christ can strengthen the weak, unstable will. Christ can exalt and purify the feeling. Christ can deepen the undeepened heart. He can possess you with His divine resources for a full, abundant, and victorious life, and in that possession there is peace. Peace is harmony. Peace is intense life. Peace is being equal to the problem. Peace is possessing adequate resources for overcoming and abundant life. *That* is the kind of peace which Jesus gives, not a dull and joyless resignation, but all the resources a guilty sinner needs to enjoy *now* eternal life "in Him."

"The valleys . . . are covered over with corn" (Ps. 65:13).

4

Harvest Thanksgiving

One of the uses of the harvest festival is to waken us to things we take for granted. We are always in peril of taking things for granted, especially in organized communities. The tinker,[1] tramping along the highway can never take his firewood for granted; nor can the desert traveler take his water, so he has to shape his course to reach the wells. But in the city where we deal with coal merchants and have water supplied to every house, such things cause us no concern at all. That is especially true of daily bread. The loaf on the table we just take for granted. It has been bought at the baker's or the grocer's, and beyond *that* our vision seldom goes. And then breaks in on us the harvest festival, and away at the back of all our city shops we see the golden mystery of harvest. We are awakened; we are shaken out of ruts—and do you know what one has said about these ruts? He has said that the rut only differs from the grave in that the latter is a little deeper. We are touched with the wonder of the commonplace—we feel the glory that invests the usual—and that is one office of the harvest festival.

It is this, too, I venture to suggest, that makes it preeminently a

---

1. a wandering mender of kettles and pans

Christian festival. For one of the beautiful things about our Lord was that He never took usual things for granted. The Pharisees were always doing that. They took the lilies of the field for granted. They took it for granted that if a woman was caught in sin, the God-appointed conduct was to stone her. And then came He with that dear heart of His in which there was always something of the child, and He went wandering and wondering through the world. He did not see the glory of the rare thing; He saw the glory of the familiar thing—of the tiny blossom that a babe could pluck and the ox could trample in the mire; of the sparrow and of the mustard-seed and of the sweaty and dirty little child; of the woman who was a sinner on the streets. It is a very comforting thing to bear in mind that He never takes *you* for granted. Other people are doing that continually—they have you classified and docketed in pigeon-holes. But to *Him* you are always wonderful though you be only a typist in an office and nobody would ever call you clever. Filled with the wonder of the commonplace, alive to the potencies of common people, never dreaming of taking things for granted in this so mystic and mysterious universe, *that* was the vision of the Savior, and it is to that *that* we are summoned by the recurrence of the harvest thanksgiving.

Another office of every harvest festival is to impress on us our mutual dependence. It is a call to halt a moment and reflect how we are all bound up with one another. Long ago in prehistoric times it was everybody for himself. Every man was his own harvester; every man was his own baker. And one may say with the most perfect confidence that if man had never risen above that, he would have been swept out of existence like the dinosaur. He survived because his Maker taught him the priceless secret of cooperation— cooperation is God's secret of survival. The bees survive in their organized communities when the ichthyosaurus is extinct. The ants survive in their interwoven polity when the screaming pterodactyl is a memory. And God who ever loved His children even before the foundation of the world taught *them* that inestimable secret. Somehow, somewhere, man learned the lesson of cooperation—learned that the one needs everybody, and that everybody needs the one— and so rose through clans into communities where there is a brotherhood of service in an infinite diversity of need.

Now at every harvest festival how vividly is that thought brought before us! It preaches with a kind of silent eloquence the interdependent brotherhood of man. Those sheaves of corn that stand within the sanctuary—who plowed the fields for them? Who in the bleak morning sowed the seed that sower and reaper might rejoice together? There are unknown plowmen and Canadian harvesters and millers and bakers whose names are never heard behind that common loaf upon the table. Was not that why the Master chose the *bread* to be the symbol of His dying love? He might have chosen one of the flowers which charmed Him and which He has bidden us consider. But choosing bread, He chose the staff of life, and that life *not* one of isolation but of a rich cooperating brotherhood. We are always in danger of forgetting that when we look at the loaf upon our table. We are always in danger of forgetting it when we buy the loaf at the baker's or the grocer's. And then the Church comes with her harvest festival and says (like Ophelia), *"This for remembrance,"*[2] and we feel the interdependence of humanity.

The third office of the harvest festival is to impress on us our utter dependence upon God. And in great communities that is another thing we are always in peril of ignoring. We are so apt to forget in cities that it is *God* who supplies our returning wants. We fall into the shallow way of thinking that *that* is the business of the shops. And we need, recurrently, to be reminded that behind everything the shops supply us with stands the shadow of the Creator. We hang on Him as utterly as a child upon its mother's breast. For every bit of food and clothing we are ultimately dependent upon Him. And to make us feel that vividly amid the supplies of organized communities is the greatest office of the harvest thanksgiving.

---

2. From *Hamlet* by William Shakespeare (1564–1616).

"These . . . have been comfort unto me"
(Col 4:11).

5

Folk Who Are a Comfort to Us

The word comfort in our text is a very interesting word. This is the only place where it occurs in the books of the New Testament. It is quite another word the Lord uses when He speaks of the Holy Spirit, the Comforter. When He says, "I will not leave you comfortless" (John 14:18), that, too, is an entirely different word. The term which is used here, and here alone in the whole range of the New Testament, is our English word *paregoric*. Now paregoric in Greek just as in English is one of the accepted terms of medicine. Paregoric is a doctor's word. And one likes to think that the Apostle Paul in his employment of such a word as this betrays, it may be quite unconsciously, the influence of the beloved physician Luke. I suppose that every real friendship has an influence upon the words we use. When we admire anybody very much, we often find their words upon our lips. And Paul, who like so many other people had an intense admiration for his doctor, would naturally use the words of Luke.

And certainly he could not have used a more appropriate or delightful word. Are you aware what paregoric means? I consulted my English dictionary to see how paregoric was defined, and I found that paregoric was a medicine that mitigates or alleviates pain. And what could be more delightful than the thought that there are men and women who are just like that—they mitigate or alleviate our pain. Pain is one of the conditions of our being. Pain is something nobody escapes. All life is rich in pain, as the throat of the bird in the spring is rich in song—the pain of striving, the pain of being baffled, the pain of loneliness and incompleteness, the pain of being misunderstood. There are people who augment that pain, sometimes without meaning it. How often is the pain of life increased by those unfortunate people who mean well. But who has not numbered in his list of friends somebody whose Christlike ministry has been to alleviate the pain of life? Such were the apostle's paregoric. Such are the paregoric of us all—often humble people, not in the least distinguished and not at all conspicuous for intellect—yet somehow in the wear and tear of life, amid its crosses and its sorrows, mitigating and alleviating pain.

Often those who alleviate life's pain, who are paregoric in the apostle's sense, are the members of our family circle, the dear ones who dwell with us at home. There was a time in Principal Rainy's[1] life when he was the most-hated man in Scotland. Scarce a week passed in which the newspapers had not some venomous attack upon him. And all the time, neither in face nor temper did Rainy show one trace of irritation, but carried himself with a beautiful serenity. One day Dr. Whyte[2] met him and said, "Rainy, I cannot understand you. How do you manage to keep serene like this, exposed to all these venomous attacks?" And Rainy answered without an instant's pause: "Whyte, *I'm very happy at home.*" The wounds were deep, but there were hands at home that were always pouring balm into the wounds—gentle, kindly ministries at home that mitigated and alleviated pain. And how many there are in every rank of life who find their courage to endure in secret, sweet comforting like that. In the perfect trust of little children, in their innocence and blessed ignorance, in the love of someone who is dear, who understands yet is always bright and hopeful, how many men have plucked up heart again, found the bitter pain of life alleviated, been strengthened for their battle with the world.

---

1. Robert Rainy (1826–1906), professor of Church History at New College, Edinburgh, United Free Church of Scotland.

2. Alexander Whyte (1837–1921), professor at New College, Edinburgh, and Free Church of Scotland clergyman.

Again, think of the comfort that we get from any friend who really understands us. Such appreciative and understanding souls—are these not the apostle's paregoric? Our Lord knew that. Never was man misunderstood as He. Misunderstood when He spoke or would not speak—misunderstood in every deed He wrought—misunderstood upon the Cross. Think of the exquisite pain of it—for that so sensitive and sinless heart fresh from the understanding of high heaven, that constant misunderstanding of mankind. And then there came an hour when Simon Peter, inspired by the Holy Spirit, cried, "Thou art the Christ, the Son of the living God" (Matt. 16:16). It thrilled our blessed Master to the depths. Life was different. He was understood. How instantly did it alleviate and mitigate all the bitter pain He had to bear. And whenever in this difficult life of ours God sends us somebody who understands, is it not always paregoric to the soul? To have somebody whom we can trust—who, we are sure, will never misinterpret—who never judges us except in love—who appreciates and understands—what earthly comfort in all the range of comfort can for one moment be compared with that?

There is one thing more I want to say, and that, too, was in the apostle's mind. Remember you can be a comfort to another though you never know anything about it. Just as the finest influence we exercise is often that of which we are unconscious, so the greatest comfort that we bring is often the comfort we know nothing of—not our preaching, nor our words of cheer, but the way in which we bear ourselves in life when the burden is heavy and the sky is black. "No man liveth to himself" (Rom. 14:7). Let men or women behave gallantly, and so behave because they trust in God, when life is difficult, when things go wrong, when health is failing, when the grave is opened; and though they may never hear a whisper of it, there are others who are thanking God for them. Every sorrow borne in simple faith is helping others bear their sorrows. Every burden victoriously carried is helping men and women to be braver. Every cross, anxiety, foreboding, shining with the serenity of trust, comes like light to those who sit in darkness. People say sometimes, "I would give anything to comfort so and so." Dear friend, if you walk in light and love, you *are* a comfort when you never know it. And other people, writing their epistle (though it will never be equal to Colossians) will put your name in, to your intense surprise, and say, "*You* were a comfort unto me."

"The Lord called Samuel. . . . And Samuel
lay until the morning, and opened the doors
of the house of the Lord" (1 Sam. 3:4, 15).

6

Vision and Duty

This was the great hour in Samuel's life. It was both his conversion and his call. We can imagine the intense excitement it must have stirred within that boyish heart. Hitherto Samuel had been a child. His farthest horizon had been his mother's home. He had been happy, as any child would be, doing his little tasks within the sanctuary. Now God had spoken to him, and called him by his name, and come into living personal contact with him, and the world of childhood had vanished like a dream. Old things had passed away; all things had become new. He had heard the voice that alters everything so that life never can be the same again. And the beautiful thing is that having heard it, Samuel lay quite quiet until the morning and then *opened the doors of the Lord's house*. It was a strange task after such a night. It accorded ill with the vision in the darkness. Was it for *him*, who had been favored so, to sweep the floor and draw aside the curtains? It is characteristic of this faithful soul that, after an hour that changed the world for him, he went back again to lowly menial duty. Voice or no voice, these doors must be opened. That was his personal and given task. No vision, however exciting or unsettling, must hinder him in his appointed office. It is a splendid trait in Samuel's character that, after the most thrilling hour of his life, he opened the doors of the Lord's house in the morning.

The same fidelity to the appointed task shines through the life of the Lord Jesus. Think, for instance, of the Transfiguration (Matt. 17:1–9; Mark 9:2–9). For Him that was an hour of vision. He was glorified in the fellowship of heaven. He saw His cross in the light of law and prophecy—for Moses and Elias spoke with Him. Could we have wondered had He lingered there in the ecstasy of heavenly vision, disdainful of the lowlier tasks of love? What a contrast between that glorious hour and the spectacle of the epileptic boy. What a change from the voices on the Mount to the uncertain voices of the crowd. And yet our blessed Lord came down the hill, and mingled with the common crowds again, and resumed His patient ministries of tenderness. *That* was His duty and His task. He was here to seek and save the lost. He was appointed to be the Good Physician of the bodies and the souls of men. And no enriching hour of heavenly vision, "above the smoke and stir of this dim spot,"[1] must keep Him from the toils of His vocation. It makes us think of Samuel in the sanctuary, faithful as a servant in God's house. He, too, had his transfiguring hour when God spoke and heaven was very near. Nonetheless, duty must be done; lowly tasks must be taken up again. He opened the doors of the Lord's house in the morning.

Now that is a lesson everyone must learn who wants to handle well the trust of life. It is hard, often, to get back to drudgery after enriching or unsettling hours. When spring has come with its strange, disturbing voices; when holidays have broadened our horizon; when love arrives, calling us by name and casting its beautiful witchery on everything, how often do the drudgeries of life which yesterday we wrought in dull content begin to seem repellent and intolerable? Sometimes, too, when a great sorrow comes, it has a like effect upon our hearts. Nothing is harder after a time of sorrow than to resume the interrupted duty. And in such hours we should remember Samuel who, when all the deeps were broken up, went quietly back to his apportioned task. To take up our common work again, to set ourselves quietly to the old drudgeries after some hour that

---

1. From "Il Penseroso" by John Milton (1608–1674).

has changed the world for us so that nothing shall be the same, that is one of the victories of life for us just as it was for Samuel, when in the morning he opened the doors of the Lord's house.

Nor must we forget this when the great vision comes of the redeeming love of God in Jesus Christ. Conversion always has its roots in vision. That vision is so wonderful that we crave something bigger than the tasks of yesterday. And often God has a larger service waiting, nor can we doubt the pointing of His will. But if it is otherwise, we must remember Samuel, and how after the voice of God had called him, he went back again to common daily duties. Great services reveal our possibilities; little services reveal our consecration. The first task of the converted man is to do better than ever what he did before. Samuel did not disdain his menial toil after the greatest hour of his life. Called and converted, he was faithful to it and *opened the doors of the Lord's house.*

"He that shall endure unto the end, the same shall be saved" (Matt. 24:13).

7

The Springs of Endurance

W e have a Scots proverb which says "He that tholes¹ overcomes." It means that he who is able to endure has learned one secret of the overcoming life. To endure is to bear patiently whatever the revolving years may bring us. It is to accept quietly and cheerfully the intractable elements of life. It is to pass through difficult or tragic hours free from any embittering of spirit, for to grow bitter is always to be beaten. We say "what can't be cured must be endured"; but that is scarcely the endurance of the Scriptures. Such endurance is a joyless thing. It is forced submission to necessity. The endurance of which the Bible speaks is of a happier character than that; it is a glad and even grateful acquiescence. Paul and Silas in the prison at Philippi did not accept things in a joyless way. They were happy; there was a lilt within their hearts; they sang so loudly that the prisoners heard them (Acts 16:25). And *that* is the endurance of the Scripture: the bearing of things in a happy kind of fashion, an acceptance with the note of triumph in it. Of that gracious and beautiful endurance the New Testament indicates three sources.

The first of these is *faith*—a burning and bright faith within the

---

1. endures

heart. That is the thought in the apostle's mind when he tells us to take the shield of faith (Eph. 6:16). A shield is not a weapon of offense. It is different from sword or spear. A shield is a protective bit of armor. It guards the soldier amid blows and buffetings. And Paul means that if we are to be guarded amid the blows and buffetings of life, there must be radiant faith within the heart. If our darker hours have no meaning in them, if they be quite devoid of plan or purpose, if there be nothing in life but accident or chance, the highest man can achieve is resignation. But if God be love, and if everything that comes to us arrives in the perfect ordering of the Father, then another temper becomes possible. He who believes that God is in the hard bit is empowered to endure the hard bit. He can say with Christ, "Even so, Father, for so it seemed good in Thy sight" (Matt. 11:26). Faith is the victory that overcomes the world. Faith finds the soul of goodness in things evil. Faith is one great secret of endurance.

Then, too, there is *love*, for love endures all things (1 Cor. 13:7). Wherever there is love within the heart, *there* is present the power to endure. Think of the mother with her little child. Not long ago she was a restless girl. *Now*, when her little one is ill, she is beautifully and divinely patient. And this endurance, which is never sullen but instinctive and often with a song in it, is the spring-token and blossoming of love. God is patient, says St. Augustine[2], because He is eternal.[2] But there is a deeper source of His patience than eternity. He is patient because He loves. He bears with and pardons us a thousand times and endures our folly and our shames just because His love endures all things. Let any man love *learning*, and what will he not endure in its acquiring? He will scorn delights and live laborious days and be supremely happy in his travail. Love is one great secret of endurance, and our Lord empowers His children to endure by the new love He kindles in their hearts. He shows them that God is eminently lovable. He reveals the lovable element in man. He sends into their hearts His gracious Spirit, and the fruit of the Spirit is love. What hatred or indifference cannot do, love can do and is doing every day. Love endures *all things*.

Lastly, there is *vision*. Moses endured as seeing Him who is invisible (Heb. 11:27). To see the invisible when skies are dark is

2. Augustine (354–430), bishop of Hippo in North Africa, early church father and philosopher.

always to have power to win through. What inspired Robert the Bruce[3] to endure? It was his vision of a liberated Scotland. What inspired Columbus to endure? It was his vision of a continent ahead. Every inventor, every explorer, every artist wrestling with his dreams endures as seeing the invisible. Never was there endurance like the Master's. It was radiant with peace and joy. It did not falter even in Gethsemane. It was equal to the agony of Calvary. And at the back of it from first to last, inspiring, animating, and sustaining it, was the unclouded vision of His Father's face. We too can practice that same presence. We can do it when life is very difficult. We can do it when the way is dark. We can do it when we cannot understand. And, doing it, we come to be so sure that underneath are the everlasting arms that endurance passes into joy.

---

3. Robert the Bruce (1274–1329), King of Scotland (1306–1329).

"Jesus. . . put forth His hand, and touched him" (Mark 1:41).

8

The Touch That Reveals

It has been said that if we want to judge a person we should never do it by a single action; but if we *must* do it by a single action, let that action be an ordinary one. A man is more likely to reveal himself in the kind of thing he habitually does than in the deed of some excited moment. Now touching is a very ordinary action. We touch a thousand things each passing day. We do not prepare ourselves for touching things as we do for the greater hours of our life. Yet in the touch of Jesus, instinctive and spontaneous, what a deal of His glory we discover! There is an evangel of the touch of Christ as surely as an evangel of the blood. I want you to think, then, of the Master's touch, that in this common ordinary action we may have some revelation of the Lord.

First, then, His touch *revealed His brotherhood*—we find that in the story of the leper. "If Thou wilt, Thou canst make me clean" (Matt. 8:2) and then we read that Jesus touched him. All that the leper expected was a cure. He thought some word of power would be pronounced. He would have been well content to light on a physician; he never dreamed he was going to find a friend. And when Jesus touched him—*him* the outcast; *him* whom everybody loathed and shunned—it was something he never could forget. He would go home and tell his wife, "He touched me." He would gather the villagers and say, "He touched me." He had found more in Christ than a physician; he had found a brother and a friend. That touch revealed to him, as nothing else could do in all the ineffable yearning of his loneliness, that he was face to face with One who understood. That was the revelation of the touch. It revealed in an instant the Savior's loving heart. It revealed His scorn of prudential morality and the self-forgetful courage of His comradeship. It was the kind of thing we are doing every day, for every day we touch a hundred objects, yet here it was the sacrament of brotherhood.

Again His touch *revealed His large authority*—it was a quietly commanding touch. That emerges with quite singular vividness in St. Luke's story of the widow of Nain (Luke 7:11–16). When He met that procession outside the city gates, the first thing He did was to address the mother. Christ has always a cheering word to say even in hours when other lips are dumb. And then Luke tells us that He touched the bier, and *immediately the whole procession halted.* He did not argue or discuss the matter. He did not beg the favor of a halt. Apparently He did not speak one syllable to the men who were carrying the bier. It was His touch that was authoritative. It was His touch that had commanding power—and His touch has commanding power to this day. How many a drunkard has that touch stopped, when heading straight for a dishonored grave! How many a woman has that touch stopped, when she was squandering the possibilities of womanhood! The touch of the Lord reveals His brotherhood, but sometimes it does more even than that. It reveals the range of His divine authority.

Then once again His touch *revealed His restfulness.* "Come unto Me and I will give you rest" (Matt. 11:28). Is not the restful touch exhibited very beautifully when there was sickness in the house of Peter? (Luke 4:28–29). Simon's mother-in-law was down with fever, of what particular kind we do not know. Her pulse was racing, and her head was aching, and she was restlessly tossing on her couch. And then, we read, the Savior came and touched her, *and immediately the fever left her.* The "storm was changed into a calm" in the house of Peter as on the Sea of Galilee. Instead of uneasy tossing there was peace. Instead of feverish unrest, repose. The infinite restfulness of Jesus flowed out through the very act of touching, and the touch itself conveyed what it revealed. There are people whose touch is wonderfully restful. That is one sure mark of a good nurse. There are people who can calm us by a touch just as others by a touch can irritate. But the touch of Jesus is unequaled, in the "fitful fever" of this life, for conveying the restfulness of God.

Lastly, His touch *revealed His uplifting power;* we see that in the case of Jairus' daughter (Mark 5:22–24, 35–43; Luke 8:41–56). When He went in the little maid was sleeping—they called it death, but Jesus called it sleep. For Him *death* meant something far more awful than the closing of those childish eyes. Then He touched her—took her by the hand—and the Gospel tells us that the maid arose; it is the elevating power of His touch. On Goldsmith's[1] monument these words are written: *nihil tetigit quod non ornavit.* They mean that within the realm of literature he touched nothing that he did not adorn. Outside literature that is not true of Oliver. He had a touch which often tarnished things. It is only true universally of Jesus. He touched water, and the water became wine, and the wine became the symbol of His blood. He touched the lilies, and their scarlet robes grew more beautiful than those of Solomon. He touched language, and common words like *talent* were lifted up from the bank into the brain. He touched Simon, and Simon became Peter. What sin touches it defiles. What the devil touches he degrades. Everything that Jesus touches is lifted up to higher, nobler levels. Of all which we have a sign and symbol when in Jairus' house that day He took the maid by the hand, *and she arose.*

---

1. Oliver Goldsmith (1730?–1774), English poet, playwrite, essayist, and novelist.

"Now the God of hope fill you with all joy
and peace in believing" (Rom. 15:13).

9

Joy and Peace in Believing

It is a question we ought to ask ourselves, in our quiet hours of
meditation, whether we really know the joy and peace which are the
benediction of our text. It is a great thing to be resigned amid the
various buffetings of life. Resignation is better than rebellion. But
resignation, however fair it be, is not peculiarly a Christian virtue; it
marks the Stoic[1] rather than the Christian. The Christian attitude
toward the ills of life is something more triumphant than acceptance. It has an exultant note that resignation lacks. It is acceptance
with a song in it. It is such a reaction on experience as suggests the
certainty of victory—the victory that overcomes the world. It is a
searching question for us all, then, whether we truly know this joy
and peace. Does it characterize our spiritual life? Is it evident in our
discipleship? And that not only on the Sabbath Day and in the
sanctuary and at the Sacrament, but in our common converse with
the world.

Contrast, for instance, joy and peace in believing with joy and

---

1. Greek philosophical school founded by Zeno (c. 340-c. 265 B.C.) stressing
inner freedom through impassiveness; principle or practice of showing indifference to pleasure or pain.

peace in working. Many who read this are happily familiar with joy
and peace in working. It is true that work may be very uncongenial;
there are those who hate the work they are engaged in. There are
seasons, too, for many of us, when strength may be unequal to the
task. But speaking generally, what a deal of joy and peace flow into
the lives of men and women in prosecuting their appointed task.
Again, think of joy and peace in loving; how evident is that in many
a home. What a peaceful and happy place a home becomes when
love lies at the basis of it all. The splendid carelessness of children,
their gladness that makes others glad, spring not only from the heart
of childhood, but from the love that encircles them at home. Now
Paul does not speak of joy and peace in working, nor does he speak
of joy and peace in loving. His theme here is different from these; it
is joy and peace in believing. And the question is, do we who know
these other things know *this* in our experience of life and amid the
jangling of our days?

Think for a moment of the men and women to whom these
words were originally written. Their cares and sorrows were just as
real to them as our cares and sorrows are to us. They were called to
be saints, and yet they were not saints. They were very far from
being saints. Some were slaves, and some were city shopkeepers,
and some were mothers in undistinguished homes. Yet Paul when
he writes to them makes no exceptions. This blessing was for every
one of them. It never occurs to him that there might be anybody
incapacitated for this joy and peace. We are so apt to think that an
inward frame like this can never be possible for *us*. We have anxieties we cannot banish; we have temperaments we cannot alter. But
just as Paul never dreamed there were exceptions in the various
temperaments he was addressing, so the Holy Spirit who inspired
the words, never dreams there are exceptions now. This is for me. It
is for you. It is for everybody who knows and loves the Lord. Not
rebellion—not even resignation when life is hard and difficult and
sorrowful—but something with the note of triumph in it; a song like
that which Paul and Silas sang; a peace that the world can never
give—and cannot take away.

Lest anyone should misread this inward frame that is the peculiar
possession of believers, note how here, as elsewhere in the Scripture, joy and peace are linked together. There is a joy that has no
peace in it. It is feverish, tumultuous, unsettled. It is too eager to be

the friend of rest, too wild to have any kinship with repose. Its true companionship is with excitement, and like other passions, it grows by what it feeds on, ever demanding a more powerful stimulus and at last demanding it in vain. There is a peace that has no joy in it. "They make a solitude and call it peace."[2] It is like a dull and sluggish river moving through an uninteresting country. But the beautiful thing is that on the page of Scripture as in the experience of the trusting soul, joy and peace are linked in closest union. The kingdom of heaven is not meat and drink; it is righteousness and joy and peace. The fruit of the Spirit is not love and joy alone; it is love and joy and peace. And our Lord, in His last great discourse when He declares His legacy of peace, closes with the triumphant note of joy. "These things have I spoken unto you" (and He had been speaking of His peace) "that your joy might be full" (John 16:24). Whom God has joined together, let not man put asunder (Matt. 19:6). There is a joy that has no peace in it. There is a peace that is dull and dead and joyless. But the mark of the followers of the Lord is the mystical marriage union of the two. It is joy *and* peace in believing.

And how eminently fitted is the Gospel message to sustain this fine reaction on experience. The Gospel is good news; it is the gladdest news that ever broke upon the ear of man. Sweet is the message of returning spring after the cold and dreariness of winter. Sweet is the message of the morning light after a night of restlessness or pain. But a thousand times sweeter, a thousand times more wonderful is the message which has been ours since we were children and which will be ours when the last shadows fall. Do we believe it? That is the vital question. Do we hold to it through the shadows and the buffetings? Do we swing it like a lamp which God has lighted over the darkest mile our feet have got to tread? Then, like joy and peace in working and in loving (with which we are all perfectly familiar), we shall experience with all the saints, joy and peace in believing.

---

2. From "Childe Harold's Pilgrimage" by George Gordon (Lord) Byron (1788–1824).

"Is not this the carpenter?" (Mark 6:3).

10

What Jesus Learned at His Trade

Every man learns certain lessons from the trade in which he is engaged. Nobody is unaffected by his business. The farmer is very different from the sailor because the one *is* a farmer and the other *is* a sailor. Each has his own outlook upon things; each dwells in his own universe. As you can often tell a man's profession by certain indications in his body, so also by indications in his soul. Now we are faced with the great fact that our blessed Savior was a carpenter. Through his youth and on to the age of thirty, Jesus was the Carpenter of Nazareth. And we may be certain, from all we know of life, that these years of carpentering would leave their mark on the public ministry of after days. They would suggest much; they would give Him certain insights; they would impress certain truths upon His mind. It was not alone in the house and in the field that He was gathering material for His teaching. He was learning things, just as we all learn them, in the quiet discharge of daily duty. These were to help Him when everything was changed. Never forget that Jesus was a poet, just as His life was God's most perfect poem. Every common task at which He worked would flash out into diamonds of significance. The village shop was not only full of logs; for Him it was also full of parables, as was His mother's kitchen and the garden and the fields.

One truth I reverently think that He would learn was how much may lie hidden in a thing. Picture the waggoner delivering a tree that had been ordered by the Carpenter of Nazareth. The Carpenter would begin to work it up; He would lop off the branches and the twigs; He would saw it into planks and blocks; He would use it for the orders He was executing. And by and by, around His little workshop would be ranged the various things that He had made—a plow, a chair, a wooden bowl or platter. What! a plow hidden in that tree, that rough, gnarled creature of the forest? And platters and bowls (to feed the children with) hidden in that swaying tree? Then the Poet-Carpenter would halt a moment and dream and say quietly to Himself, "Ah, how much may lie hidden in a thing." Did He forget that when carpentering days were over? Was not that one glorious secret of His hopefulness? He saw the Kingdom in a mustard seed. He saw the citizen of heaven in a child. He saw, as no one else has ever seen, how much lay hidden in the human heart and in the lives and characters of common men.

Another truth I believe that He would learn is what pains it takes just to transform a thing. That would be deeply graven on His heart. Picture a farmer coming to the shop and asking the Carpenter to make a plow. An Eastern plow was a very simple thing. The farmer would sit there until it was made. "Friend," the Carpenter would say to him, "my plows are not manufactured while you wait. It is a long and weary business making plows! See that tree? I have got to transform that tree. I have got to change that tree into your plow. Who can tell what faults and flaws are in it? Leave Me alone. I have to wrestle with it." With such material, so rude and so intractable, one thing the Carpenter would learn was this: that pains and patience go to all transforming. Was *that* forgotten when carpentering days were over?

Think of the first disciples. Not in one hour did Simon become Peter. John was not made an apostle "while you wait." There is nothing more wonderful in history than the long, patient, and persistent way in which the Lord transformed these followers of Galilee. In a single instant He could heal the leper. In a single instant He could raise the dead. It took many a thousand weary instants to transform Simon into Peter.

And what more beautiful training for that ministry than to be sent of God until the age of thirty to toil as the lowly Carpenter of Nazareth. Perhaps one day when things were very difficult and the disciples were like wayward children, Jesus caught sight of a plow that He had made and remembered all the pains that it had cost Him. And then He would thank His Father that He had been a carpenter, for if it took all these pains to make a plow, how infinitely more to make a Peter. We are all in the hands of One who was a carpenter. That is a fact we never should forget. He is a thorough workman. He never spares Himself. He is eager for perfection in His workmanship. And some day, when His work on *us* is over and we are perfected in His own perfect way, we shall say, "Is not *this* the Carpenter?"

Then, lastly, might He not learn in carpentering that the finest things are made of hardest wood? It was cedar-wood that was demanded for the paneling of palace or of temple. Did He smile, I wonder, when He noticed that? Did He recognize the deeper meaning of it? And was He recalling the old days in Nazareth when He deliberately selected Paul? Hard as cedar, injurious, a persecutor, the bitter and savage foe of every Christian—but finest things may be made from hardest wood. Do you know anyone who is what is called a hard case—anyone who has resisted every pleading—some member of your flock or some wild lad you try to teach on Sundays? Have faith. Some day he will be won. The cedar will adorn the temple yet. And then you will say quietly and adoringly, *"Is not this the Carpenter?"*

"Now the God of hope fill you with all joy
and peace in believing, that ye may abound
in hope, through the power of the Holy
Spirit" (Rom. 15:13).

11

The God of Hope

In the Hebrew language, as scholars know, there are several different words for rain from which we gather that in Hebrew life rain
was something of very great importance. It is the same, though in
the realm of spirit, with the names of God in the letters of St. Paul.
The variety of divine names there betrays the deepest heart of the
apostle. Think, for instance, of the names one lights on in this
fifteenth chapter of the Romans, all of them occurring incidentally.
He is the God of patience and of consolation (v. 5). I trust my
readers have all found Him that. He is the God of peace (v. 33),
keeping in perfect peace every one whose mind is stayed on Him.
He is the God of hope (v. 13), touching with radiant hopefulness
everything that He has made, from the mustard-seed to the children
of mankind.

Think, for instance, how beautifully evident is the hopefulness
of God in nature. Our Lord was very keenly alive to that. There is
much in nature one cannot understand, and no loving communion
will interpret it. There is a seeming waste and cruelty in nature
that often lies heavy on the heart. But just as everything is beautiful in nature that the hand of man had never tampered with, so

what a glorious hopefulness she breathes! Every seed cast into the soil, big with hopefulness of coming harvest. Every sparrow in the winter ivy, hopeful of the nest and of the younglings. Every brook rising in the hills and brawling over the granite in the glen, hopeful of its union with the sea. Winter comes with iciness and misery, but in the heart of winter is the hope of spring. Spring comes tripping across the meadow, but in the heart of spring there is the hope of summer. Summer comes garlanded with beauty, but in the heart of summer is the hope of autumn when sower and reaper shall rejoice together. Paul talks of the whole creation groaning and travailing in pain together. But a woman in travail is not a hopeless woman. Her heart is "speaking softly of a hope." The very word *natura* is the witness of language to that hopeful travail—it means something going to be born. If, then, this beautiful world of nature is the garment of God by which we see Him, if His Kingdom is in the mustard seed and not a sparrow can fall without His knowledge, how evident it is that He in whom we trust, who has never left Himself without a witness, is *the God of hope*.

Again, how evident is this attribute in the inspired word of the New Testament. The New Testament, as Dr. Denney[1] used to say, is the most hopeful book in the whole world. I believe that God is everywhere revealed—in every flower in the crannied wall. But I do not believe that He is everywhere *equally* revealed any more than I believe it of myself. There are things I do that show my character far more fully than certain other things—and God has made me in His image. I see Him in the sparrow and the mustard-seed; I see Him in the lilies of the field; but I see more of Him, far more of Him, in the inspired word of the New Testament. And the fine thing to remember is just this, that the New Testament is not a hopeless book. Hope surges in it. Its note is that of victory. There steals on the ear in it the distant triumph song. It closes with the Book of Revelation where the Lamb is upon the throne. And if *this* is the expression of God's being far more fully than anything in nature, how sure we may be He is *the God of Hope*.

And then, lastly, we turn to our Lord and Savior. Is not He the most magnificent of optimists? Hope burned in Him (as Lord

---

1. James Denney (1856–1917), Scottish Free Church theologian.

Morley[2] said of Cromwell[3]) when it had gone out in everybody else. There is an optimism based on ignorance: not such was the good hope of Christ. With an eye that sin had never dulled, He looked in the face all that was dark and terrible. There is an optimism based on moral laxity: not such was the good hope of Christ. He hated sin, although He loved the sinner. Knowing the worst, hating what was evil, treated by men in the most shameful way, Christ was gloriously and sublimely hopeful until death was swallowed up in victory; hopeful for the weakest of us, hopeful for the very worst, hopeful for the future of the world. Now call to mind the word He spoke: *"He that hath seen me, hath seen the Father"* (John 14:9). He that has seen into that heart of hopefulness has seen into the heart of the Eternal. Once a man has won that vision, though there are many problems that may vex him still, he never can doubt again through all his years, the amazing hopefulness of God.

---

2. John (Viscount) Morley of Blackburn (1838–1923), English statesman, biographer, journalist and critic.

3. Oliver Cromwell (1599–1658), Puritan statesman, Lord Protector of England 1653–1658.

"In the shadow of His hand hath He hid
me" (Isa. 49:2).

12

The Shadow of His Hand

The hand of God in Scripture is very often comfortingly mentioned. It is one of the great sources of the strength and solace of His people. It is a hand of almighty power, for it takes up the islands as a very little thing. It is a hand of unfailing liberality, for it supplies all our returning wants. It is a hand of beauty and of wisdom, for it arrays the lilies of the field and leads the wandering feet into green pastures. It is that hand of which the prophet says, "In the shadow of His hand hath He hid me." Now there is a deep sense in which every believer leads a *continuously* hidden life. It is a life "hid with Christ in God" (Col. 3:3), and that from the beginning to the close. But the concealment of which the prophet speaks is not the constant abiding in the Father; it is the temporary sheltering of His love.

There are times in every spiritual life when the greatest of all needs is quiet withdrawal. For the spiritual harvesting of life, shadow is as needful as the sunshine. And it is one of the great offices of faith to take the shadowed seasons of the life and to reckon them the shadow of His hand. It is not the whole of faith to be assured that God's hand is guiding through the years. Hours come when we are laid aside, secluded and withdrawn from high activities. And in such hours it is a mighty comfort if faith is strong enough so to transmute the shadows that they become the shadow of His hand. Sometimes He hides us in the shadow of His hand that the little flickering light be not extinguished. A bruised reed He will not break and smoking flax He will not quench (Isa. 42:3; Matt. 12:20). When a taper has been newly kindled, the slightest gust of wind will put it out. It is then that a man, to guard it from extinction, will encircle it with the shadow of his hand. And often, when the heavenly light is lit and not yet equal to the whirling wind, God shelters it in some such way as that (Acts 9:30; Gal. 1:17). That was why Paul was sent into Arabia after the great hour of his conversion. That is why (as Mr. Spurgeon[1] puts it) God often refuses first offers of service. That is why He puts us in our homes in the secluded and sheltered days of childhood when things unseen are so intensely real. That hiding of the apostle in Arabia, that blessed seclusion of our infancy, that secrecy which distinguishes beginnings whether of a daisy or a soul, all of it is the stratagem of love that the smoking flax be not extinguished. It is God's hiding in the shadow of His hand.

Sometimes He hides us in the shadow of His hand that life may be deepened and enriched. Think, for instance, of the case of Luther.[2] Luther had reached the climax of his life; his influence was mighty across Europe. And just then his life was split apart he was shut up in the old German fortress. Yet who can doubt now, as he recalls the story and remembers all that it involved and led to, that for Luther the shadow of that fortress was the shadow of the hand of God? He came forth deepened and enriched. He came forth newly armored in the Word. He came forth with a new serenity and under a heaven that held a larger sovereignty. And how many are there who have been withdrawn, it may be in the flood-tide of activities, to find afterward, as Luther found, that they have gained more than they have lost? All life is dark with shadows. Are they not often very enriching shadows? Have they not taught us what we never learned when the sun was blazing in the sky? So we look back on things that in their coming fretted us and made us wonder if God was really

---

1. Charles H. Spurgeon (1834–1892), influential English Baptist preacher.
2. Martin Luther (1483–1546), German theologian and leader of Protestant Reformation.

Love, and *now* we recognize with perfect clearness that they were all the shadow—of His hand.

Again He hides us in the shadow of His hand in the interests of a larger service. We are withdrawn from things that we are doing because He has better things for us to do. How strange it must have seemed to Paul that he should languish in a Roman jail. Was it not intolerable, that confinement, and he on fire to evangelize the world? Yet some of the greatest of his letters that are read today in Africa and China would never have been written but for that. Very often the way to richer service lies through a season of seclusion. Illness comes, or unexpected trial, or the bitter anguish of bereavement. And then we discover, as the years pass, how new notes have stolen into the music, often the very notes the world was wanting. It is a wonderful thing to be *guided* by God's hand and to feel it increasingly with the increasing years. That was profoundly felt by the apostle as it was profoundly felt by Bunyan.[3] Yet some of the richest letters of St. Paul and the *Pilgrim's Progress* of John Bunyan come to us from the shadow of His hand. It is the glory of God to hide a thing, and He has a thousand places where He hides things. Some He hides in the bosom of the earth, and others, like pearls beneath the sea. But His children are far more precious to Him than the costliest of pearls or diamonds, and He hides *them* in the shadow of His hand.

If this is true of all who trust Him, it is preeminently true of Christ. He is the author and finisher of faith. One thinks of His preexistence when He was hidden from our mortal eyes. One thinks of the long years at Nazareth where He had His dwelling in such deep seclusion. One thinks of the quiet garden-grave where He was hidden even from His own, beyond the reach of any earthly ministry. So is it at this present hour. Our blessed Lord is ours in faith alone. Hidden from us is that glorious form still bearing the mystic traces of its agony. But it is not the shadows of the centuries that hide Him nor the darker shadows of the tomb. *He is hidden in the shadow of God's hand.*

---

3. John Bunyan (1628–1688), English Nonconformist preacher and author of *Pilgrim's Progress.*

"They took Him even as He was" (Mark 4:36).

13

Taking Him as He Was

From the first verse of this chapter we infer that Christ had been teaching the people from the boat. He was not particular about His pulpit. He had sat in the ship a little way from land and spoken so to the crowds upon the shore. Now the teaching was over; He was weary; He was craving for a period of rest. And so He bade His disciples cross the lake, and that is the moment to which our text refers—they took Him even as He was. Perhaps the sky was threatening a storm, and someone had suggested fetching cloaks. Or one had hinted at getting a store of food if they were going to camp out on the other side. And then Peter, who was dictating this, recalled a certain eagerness in Christ so that all the kindly hints had come to nothing. They had not waited until any cloaks were brought. They had not sent a messenger ashore. Weary and probably hungry, they had taken Him even as He was. That is a great task for all of us, and I should like to consider for a little some of the many folk who fail to do it.

First, then, I speak of those *who take Jesus as they think He ought to be*. It is the temptation of many godly people, and that is the reason why I put it first. They never doubt that Jesus is divine. Their confessing cry is that of Thomas. Then they remember what they learned in childhood, that God sees everything and is omni-

53

scient. And so, quite independently of Scripture and as an inference
from the attributes of God, they conclude that it was so with Him.
Then perhaps they open Scripture, and they find Him saying, "I do
not know." Or they read that He was astonished and surprised, and,
of course, omniscience never is surprised. And it perplexes them
and gives them arrowy doubts as if the writers were tampering with
their Lord and laying violent hands upon His glory. Then comes the
temptation to wrest Scripture, and to make it mean what it could
never mean, and to evade the sense that any child would gather if
you put the Bible in his hand. And to all such I would say quietly
and very gently (for I honor them), "Friend, you must take Him
even as He was." Never dream that you are honoring God by im-
posing your conceptions upon God. Never dream that any thoughts
of yours can be worthier than those the Bible gives you. You are a
child, a learner, a disciple, and as a child you must come to Christ in
Scripture. You must take Him even as He was.

That this is the only way to get to know Christ I might illustrate
in simple fashion. I might think of the knowledge we have gained
of nature. For long centuries men came to nature with certain pre-
conceptions in their minds. They had their theories about the world,
and to these theories nature must conform. And the result was
ignorance and rank empiricism and a science that was falsely so
called and the countless errors of the Middle Ages. Then came
Bacon[1]—and what did Bacon do? He took *nature* even as she was.
He swept away that fog of preconception. He accepted facts as
simply as a child. And the result was a real and growing insight into
the mystery of God in nature which has illuminated all the world
for us. For us the wayside weed is wonderful, and the tiniest insect
is composed of miracle. For us there is a glory in the heavens such
as was never dreamed of by the Psalmist. And all that knowledge
has been brought to us because these gallant toilers of the dawn had
the courage to take nature *as she was.*

Again, I think of those *who take Him as they find Him in the
books they read.* Our modern literature is full of Christ even though
His name is never mentioned. There is a Christ of Browning[2] and of

---

1. Roger Bacon (1214?–1294?), English philosopher and scientist.
2. Elizabeth Barrett Browning (1806–1861), English poet.

Tennyson.[3] There is a Christ of Mr. Wells.[4] There is a Christ of the novels of George Eliot,[5] and of the sermons of Newman[6] and of Spurgeon.[7] Yet all these are but imperfect paintings, and the yearning heart can never rest in them. To know Him and to trust Him and to love Him we must take Him *even as He was.* That was what the wise men from the East did. In their books they had been told of Him. And then the star appeared and led them to the cradle—and the cradle was but a sorry manger. Many a scholar would have gone home again, preferring his scholarly dreams to this reality; but *they* took Him even as He was. Took Him in the manger with the ox and ass as His companions—gave Him the gold and frankincense and myrrh—worshiped and adored. These students of all the learning of the Orient did what every student has to do—they took Him even as He was.

Lastly, I think of those *who take Him as they see Him in the lives of others.* Someone has very truly said that a Christian is the Bible of the street. There are multitudes who judge of Christ by what they see in His professing followers. And very often that is a noble witness, fraught with an influence incalculable and rich in commendation of the Master. A godly and consecrated father is a noble argument for Christ. A Christlike mother in a home full of cares is more convincing than any book of evidences. But the pity is that you and I who trust Him are often so very different from that. And to all who are watching *us* and judging Him by *us,* and scorning Him perhaps for what they see in *us,* I say, "Friend, you are not dealing fairly with the Master. You must take Him *even as He was.*" You would never dream of judging Chopin[8] by the schoolgirl's rendering on her poor piano. Is it perfectly fair to judge of Christ by the imperfect rendering of His learners? What a difference it would make for multitudes if only, like the disciples on the lake, they would take Him even as He was.

---

3. Alfred (Lord) Tennyson (1809–1892), English poet.

4. H. G. Wells (1866–1946), English novelist and historian.

5. George Eliot (Mary Ann Evans) (1819–1880), English novelist.

6. John Henry Cardinal Newman (1801–1890), English theologian and author.

7. Charles H. Spurgeon (1834–1892), influential English Baptist preacher.

8. Frederic Chopin (1810–1849), Polish composer and pianist, in France after 1831.

"He that seeth Me seeth Him that sent Me"
(John 12:45).

14

Seeing Jesus, Seeing God

That these words are of profound importance we may gather from two considerations. The one is that our Savior *cried* them (v. 44). As a rule our Savior did not cry. He would not cry nor lift up His voice in the streets. But now and then in some exalted hour the Gospels tell us that He cried (John 7:37). And in every instance when He cried we have an utterance of transcendent moment that takes us to the very heart of things. Then we must not forget that in these verses we have our Lord's last public sermon. From the beginning of the next chapter onward, our Lord is in seclusion with His own. And we may be certain that every word He uttered in His final and farewell discourse would be fraught with an infinite significance.

We recognize that infinite significance when we face the problem of our faith today. Our problem is not to believe there is a God but to be sure that He answers to our highest thought of Him. We may justly and seriously question if if any man is really an atheist. Some think they are in moments of recoil; others assert it on the Hyde Park[1] platform. But it seems to me that the thought of God is intermingled with our deepest being, as the sunshine is intermingled

---

1. A public park in London where open speeches and debates take place.

with the daffodils which are making the world beautiful just now. Our difficulty is not to believe there is a God. The atheist has been replaced by the agnostic. Our real difficulty centers in His character—is He equal to our highest thought of Him? For when life is difficult and ways are shadowed, the soul can never have quietness and confidence unless the Rock is "higher than I."

This difficulty is profoundly felt in the modern study of the world of nature. "I find no proof in nature," wrote Huxley[2] once to Kingsley,[3] "of what you call the fatherhood of God." Nature is quick with whisperings of God as every lover of her knows. That was one reason why our Savior loved her and haunted the places where the lilies were. But no one can seriously study nature without finding there elements of cruelty, and at once the thoughtful mind begins to ask, "Is there, then, cruelty in God?" If there is, He may be still "the Rock," but He is not "the Rock that is higher than I" (Ps. 61:2). We never can trust Him in an entire surrender if there is a shadow of cruelty in His nature. And that is the difficulty of many students now, *not* to disbelieve existence of a God, but to believe that He is higher than our highest.

Or, again, we turn to human life, eager to find God in human life. That is a perfectly reasonable inquiry, for "in Him we live and move and have our being" (Acts 17:28). Now, tell me, when we turn to human life, are there not things in it that look like gross injustices? Injustices that do not spring from character nor from any harvesting of sin? And if man is not responsible for these, at once the thinking mind begins to ask, "Is it God, then, who is responsible for these?" Granted that He is, God may still exist. Atheism is an illogical conclusion. But granted that He is, how can we ever love Him with our whole soul and strength and mind? If in Him in whom we have our being there is the faintest suspicion of injustice, we never can trust Him in utter self-surrender. Take everything you find in life and nature and transfer it to the heart upon the throne, and how extraordinarily difficult it is to believe that the Rock is higher than ourselves. And yet unless it is infinitely higher, there is no help for us when the golden bowl is broken, nor when the daughters of music are brought low (Eccl. 12:4, 6).

---

2. Thomas Henry Huxley (1825–1895), English biologist and writer.
3. Charles Kingsley (1819–1875), English clergyman, novelist and poet.

And then we hear the word of the Lord Jesus, "He that beholdeth *Me* beholdeth Him that sent Me." Or, as He said to Philip only a little later, "He that hath seen Me hath seen the Father" (John 14:9). We are *not* commanded to take all we find in nature or in life and carry it up to the heart upon the throne. "What I do thou knowest not now, but thou shalt know hereafter" (John 13:7). But we *are* commanded, over and over again, to take everything we find in Jesus and by *that* to read the character of God. Just as a little moorland pool will reflect all the glory of the heavens, so Christ in the limits of His humiliation is the mirror of the heart of God. That is what the writer to the Hebrews means when at the beginning of his magnificent epistle he calls Christ the "reflection of His glory" (1:3). That is a very splendid act of faith in this seemingly unjust and cruel world. But that is the act of faith which marks the Christian. We *by Him* do believe in God (1 Peter 1:21). If he who has seen Christ has seen the Father, then we can trust the Father to the uttermost and leave all other difficulties to be cleared when the day breaks and the shadows flee away.

"My spirit is overwhelmed within me; my heart within me is desolate" (Ps. 143:4).

15

When the Spirit Is Overwhelmed

There are some natures more exposed than others to this overwhelming of the spirit, but it would be untrue to life to say that the peril can be limited to temperament. Some of the last people one would ever dream of are prone to this hopeless sinking of the heart. The author of "The Christian Year"[1] was a man of singular serenity; he had a happy humility of soul; he delighted in the beauty of the world. Yet in one of his letters to Sir John Coleridge[2] he tells us of the fight he had to wage against this overwhelming of the spirit. I should look for it in Jeremiah, that most tremulous of all the prophets; but in Elijah—that man of iron will—I should scarcely anticipate the finding of it. Yet in the life of Elijah came an hour when, plunged into the deeps, his prayer was that God would let him die (1 Kings 19:4). There are few things that men hide so well as this interior desolation. Brave folk are adept in concealing it. It is when men and women meet us brightly, though there be not a star in all their sky, that we feel the heroism of humanity.

---

1. John Keble (1792–1866), English clergyman and poet.
2. Sir John Coleridge (1790–1876), English jurist and writer.

Sometimes this overwhelming comes for reasons that are purely physical. This is the body of our humiliation, and we are fearfully and wonderfully made. I asked a friend only the other evening if she knew the overwhelmed spirit, and she answered, "Only when I am very, very tired." Women especially get so very tired. In Spenser's[3] "Faërie Queene" there is a magnificent description of Despair, and the fine touch is that the knight confronts Despair when he has been a prisoner in a dungeon. Give him his charger, let him ride abroad, fill his lungs with the fresh air of heaven, and he never meets the horrid form of hopelessness. Nothing is more delicate and subtle than the interaction of the body and the soul. Lack of faith is sometimes lack of oxygen which should make us very tenderhearted and forbearing and compassionate in judgment toward those who are never really well.

Sometimes, again, this overwhelming comes through the congregating of our troubles. Troubles never come singly, says the proverb. One remembers how in the Book of Job the messengers come hot-foot on each other. Another and another and another, and each of them with his tale of evil tidings. The dramatic touch is that each of them arrives *before the other has done speaking*, and how true that is to human life! Did bitter things come at equal intervals there would be time for the reinforcing of the soul. We could collect ourselves and summon our reserves if the onsets were distributed like that. But who does not know how, when anything goes wrong, *everything* that day seems to go wrong, until often when it rings to evensong, the spirit is overwhelmed within us.

Sometimes, again, this overwhelming comes through failure to do one's simple duty. To shirk one's God-appointed task is to court the presence of despair. When Bunyan's Christian and Hopeful were in the King's Highway, Giant Despair never was encountered. But when they crossed the stile and got into By-path Meadow, *then* they fell into the giant's clutches. And whenever anybody leaves the King's Highway and crosses the stile into By-path Meadow, sooner or later, but relentlessly, "melancholy marks him for her own." What did Wordsworth[4] say of the man who does his duty? He said, "Flowers laugh before him in their beds." The whole world

---

3. Edmund Spenser (1552–1599), English poet.
4. William Wordsworth (1770–1850), English poet.

grows radiant and musical when we are true to the footsteps of our Lord. To omit the task we know we ought to do, to shirk the demanded duty of the hour, to shun the cross, to refuse to lift the burden, to put selfishness in place of service, all this in this strange life of ours is to head straight for the overwhelmed spirit.

I should like, too, to say just here that we should never pass judgment in overwhelmed hours. Let a man accept the verdict of his Lord, but never the verdict of his melancholy. Hours come when everything seems wrong, and when all the lights of heaven are blotted out, and how often in such desolate hours do we fall to judging the universe and God! It is part of the conduct of the instructed soul to resist that as a temptation of the devil and to refuse the verdict of its melancholy. Such hours are darkened hours, and the judgments of darkness are always unreliable. The things that frighten us in the night are the things we smile at in the morning. We are like that traveler among the hills of Wales who in the mist thought he saw a specter; when it came nearer, he found it was a man; when it came up to him, it was his brother. Overwhelmed times are times for leaning; God does not mean them to be times for judging. They are given us for striking out; they are not given us for summing up. Leave that until the darkness has departed, and the "rosy-fingered dawn"[5] is on the hills, and in His light we see light again.

For the great need of hours of overwhelming is the old, old need of trust in God. It is to feel, as the little children's hymn has it, that we are "safe in the arms of Jesus." To be assured that God is love and that He will never leave us nor forsake us (Matt. 28:20); to be assured that He knows the way we take and that His grip is on us all the time, *that* is the way to keeping a brave heart when everything is dark and desolate and not a bird is singing in the forest. Plunged into the deeps, there is something deeper than these deeps. There is the love of God commended in the cross. *Underneath* are the everlasting arms (Deut. 33:27). So we endure as seeing the invisible, and then (and often sooner than we look for) the day breaks and the shadows flee away (Song of Sol. 2:17).

---

5. From the *Odyssey* attributed to Homer (850 B.C.?).

"As the Father hath loved Me, so have I loved you" (John 15:9).

16

The Great Comparison

That their blessed Master loved them was one thing which the disciples never doubted. It was the crowning glory of their years. There are those who always find it easy to believe that other people love them. They accept love, as the flowers accept the sunshine in an entirely natural and happy way. But there are some who find it very hard just to be certain that other people love them, and one or two of the disciples were like that. Our Lord had to deal with very various temperaments in that extraordinary little company. Some were responsive and receptive; others, like Thomas, wanted proof of things. And yet there was one thing that they never doubted through all the change and variations of the years, and that was that their Master loved them. The *fact* was evident to every heart, and yet behind the fact they felt a mystery. There was something different in the love of Jesus from all the human love that they had known. No love of wife, nor of any precious child, nor of friend, nor of father, nor of mother fully interpreted the Master's love. *It* did what these had never done. It demanded what these had never asked. It spoke sometimes with an unearthly accent quite alien from that of human love. They were baffled occasionally and perplexed, so profoundly new was the experience that came to them in the love of the Lord Jesus. It was then that Jesus made this great comparison that threw such a vivid light on everything. "As the Father hath loved Me, *so* have I loved you." And long afterward when hours of darkness came and they were tempted to wonder if He loved them still, what comfort must these words have brought them!

They would recall, for instance, how the Father's love for Christ inspired Him for the service of mankind. It was the Father's love that sent Him to the world not to be ministered unto but to minister. Human love is often prone to selfishness. It wants to grasp the dear one and to keep him. It shrinks from the thought of charging the beloved with any embassy whose end is death. Yet on such an embassy whose issue was a cross, God sent not any angel but His Son—*and the Son was certain that the Father loved Him.* Inspiring all His service for mankind, quickening Him for every lowly ministry, holding Him to His appointed task was His profound conviction of His Father's love. And then, on that last night of earthly fellowship, He turned to His disciples with the words, "As the Father hath loved Me, *so* have I loved you." How these words would come back to them again in their evangelization of the world! It was love that had given them their work to do no matter how difficult or perilous. And to find in our work, however hard it is, an argument for the love of the Lord Jesus is one of the quiet triumphs of the spirit. His is not a love that gives us ease any more than the love of the Father gave Him ease. It sends us out, morning after morning, to a service which may be only drudgery. And what illumines duty and warms its chilly hands and brings a song into the heart of it is the certainty of love behind it all. It made all the difference to Christ that the Father's love had given Him the task. It made the task a love-gift and touched it as with the joy of heaven. And then He says to all His toiling followers in every century and country, "As the Father hath loved Me, *so* have I loved you."

They would recall again how the Father's love for Christ did not exempt Him from the sorest suffering. He was the well-beloved Son yet a man of sorrows and acquainted with grief. If there is one thing we all crave to do, it is to shield our loved ones from the sting of pain. That passion is in the heart of every mother as she clasps to her breast her little child. Yet here was a love of the Father for the Son that gave the Son, and did it quite deliberately, to bitter suffering ending in a cross. Often when our beloved suffer we are powerless. We know the agony of being helpless. We have to witness excruciating pain, impotent to do anything that might relieve it. But the Father, clothed in His omnipotence, with a single word could have put an end to suffering—and yet He loved His Son and did not do it.

I wonder if the disciples thought of that when afterward they recalled this word of Jesus. Stoned, shipwrecked, persecuted, tortured, could it be possible their Master loved them still? And then, clear as a silver bell, these words would strike upon their ears again, "As the Father hath loved Me, *so* have I loved you." *He* was loved, and yet He suffered sorely. He was loved, and yet His face was marred. He was loved with an everlasting love, and yet all the billows of this mortal life went over Him. What an unspeakable comfort for these gallant souls, tempted through suffering to arrowy doubt, this *as* and *so* of the Lord Jesus. All God's children must remember that, when they are tempted so to doubt the love of heaven. Have not many cried beside some bed of agony, "How can God be love if He permits this?" In such an hour argument is powerless, but there is one Voice that is never powerless. It is His who suffered—and was loved.

They would recall, too, that the Father's love for Christ was a love that justified itself at last. There came at last the hour of resurrection and of ascension to the right hand in heaven. Was it love that gave Him to the earth? It was love that lifted Him above the earth. Was it love that permitted Him to suffer? It was love that crowned His sufferings in glory. The final issue of the Father's love was not the quietness of a garden-grave. It was song; it was dominion; it was liberty. What a magnificent hope for these disciples, persecuted and in prison. What a magnificent hope for every disciple just when things are growing unendurable! A little patience and the love that grips us is going to justify itself magnificently. *That* is bound, as with hoops of steel, to the *as* and *so* of the Lord Jesus.

"The rich and poor meet together: the Lord is the maker of them all" (Prov. 22:2).

17

Meeting Places

Of the meeting-places between rich and poor, the earliest is the *cradle*. In happy childhood when heaven lies about us, social distinctions are unknown. Between two men a great gulf may be set in the separations of society. One may wear the coronet of rank and the other be a humble laborer. And yet when they were children long ago, perhaps not even Jonathan and David were more trusty friends than were these little souls. They played together, built forts together, fought together, and were supremely happy. They were one in community of interests not less than in comradeship of hearts. And the rich and the poor met together *there*, for the Lord was the maker of them all.

Again, one remembers how they meet *in the possession of a common nature*. In the deep places of our human hearts there are touches of nature that make the whole world kin. Rich Joseph falls upon dead Jacob's face in the bitter sorrow of a father's passing (Gen. 50:1). King David, brokenhearted, cries, "Would God I had died for thee, O Absalom, my son!" (2 Sam. 18:33). Yet open the door of the poorest home in Britain, where the chair is empty and the coffin full, and there is the same sad music of humanity. I should expect the rich to be enamored of life, for on them life has

lavished of its best. But the very poor, herded in the slum—would
you reckon that *they* could be enamored so? Yet the passion for life
burns with as keen a flame in the destitute as in the opulent, and in
these elemental things we are akin. Does love only enter at the
castle gates? Does it never look in of a morning at the cottage
window? Is memory the possession of a class? Is imagination to be
bought in markets? God breaks our social distinctions down in the
impartial scattering of gifts like these, and the rich and poor meet
together there.

Again one notes, with ever-deepening wonder, how they meet
together *at the feet of Christ*. That is so written on the gospel story
that he who runs may read (Hab. 2:2). These were times of bitter
social cleavage imperiling the whole fabric of society. It was a
religious cleavage before it was a social one, and that is the most
ominous of all. And then came Jesus, drawing to His feet the
children of every separated section, Mediator between sundered
classes as truly as between God and man. Rich men like Nicodemus sought Him. Poor men like Simon Peter loved Him passionately. Women ministered to Him of their substance, and the beggars
by the highway waited for Him. One came to Him with the request that He would settle some dispute about inheritance, and
scores who had no inheritance at all. So has it been right down the
course of history. Slave and emperor have knelt together. Rich
young rulers have come running to Him and found the indigent
were there before them. In every land where Jesus has been
preached, the rich and the poor have met together *there*, for that
Lord is the maker of them all.

Nor must we forget that what is true of Jesus is true of *everyone who really follows Him*. We have that very beautifully put in
one of the expressions of St. Paul. Writing to the Corinthians he
says, "Henceforth know we no man after the flesh" (2 Cor. 5:16).
That does *not* mean that after his conversion he had withdrawn
himself from social intimacies. It means that after he had found
the Lord, his former superficial social judgments were among the
old things that had passed away. Once, in his unconverted days,
Paul had judged with the judgment of the world. He had valued
men for ability or brilliance. He had reckoned their worth by
station or by wealth. Now, converted, everything was altered; the
old values had gone whistling down the wind; in Christ there was

neither rich nor poor. Perhaps there is no time when one feels that more than in the quiet hour of a Scots Communion. There sits my lord, and in the pew beside him, handling the same elements, the plowman. Something has happened. Someone has been abroad smashing down the barriers of class. And the rich and poor meet together *there*.

Then, lastly, one quietly meditates on this, that they meet together *at the end*. For there is one house appointed for all living, and after death, the judgment. In every theater of every city there are several doors of entrance and of exit. This mirrored passage is for the moneyed folk. That rough stone stair is for the crowd. So in the theaters of men are all sifted and sorted by the purse. Not so in the theater of God. In that there is but one entrance and one exit. For all are born, and for us all, at last, it is dust unto dust and ashes unto ashes. *And then?* "And I saw a great white throne and Him that sat on it, from whose face the earth and the heaven fled away. And I saw the dead, small and great, stand before God" (Rev. 20:11). There all stand alike. The poorest shall have that mighty Advocate than whom the richest cannot have a better. And the rich and poor shall meet together *there*, for the Lord is the maker of them all.

"Simon, I have somewhat to say unto thee" (Luke 7:40).

18

Somewhat to Say

It is one of the notable things about our Lord that always He has somewhat to say. No hour of need ever finds Him silent. The intrusion of the woman into Simon's dining-room was an entirely unexpected incident. It was a painful and perplexing moment when she made her way into the feast. But our Lord had somewhat to say then, and one of the wonderful things about Him is that, always, He has somewhat to say still. Listen to the speaker at the street corner discussing Socialism or industrial unrest. Join an eager company of young people gathered to reconstitute the universe. Socrates and Shakespeare are not mentioned, but almost always Christ is summoned in—they all feel He has somewhat to say still. Heaven and earth have passed away, but His words have not passed away. We live under a different heaven now, and the earth has been displaced from her centrality. Yet still, on every problem which emerges, Jesus Christ has somewhat to say. It is a fact which is well worth considering.

He has somewhat to say, it should be noted, *just when everybody else is silent.* My impression is that when that woman entered, you might have heard a pin drop in the dining-room. Some of the guests would hang their heads, and some would look at each other "with a wild surmise." A sudden quiet would fall upon the table; conversation would instantly be hushed. And just then, when there was silence, when nobody else had a syllable to utter, our Lord had somewhat to say. So was it in the house of Jairus when the father and mother could do naught but weep (Luke 8:41–56; Mark 5:22–24, 35–43). So was it outside the gates of Nain when the widow was stricken dumb in her great sorrow (Luke 7:11–16)—and the wonderful thing is that so is it still. When all the philosophers are dumb and cannot give one word of help or comfort; when learning has no message to inspire or to console the heart; when sympathy hesitates to break the silence lest it give "vacant chaff well-meant for grain,"[1] the Lord has something to say. Nothing can rob Him of His message, not even the bitterest experience of life. He never grows silent when the way is dark nor when the feet go down into the valley. There are many voices and none without significance; but the hour comes when they all fail us, and then we find how in such hours as that, Jesus has somewhat to say.

One notes, too, that He has somewhat to say to those *separated from Him by great distances*. What a gulf there was between our Lord and Simon! It is true that Jesus was sitting next to Simon for that was the place of the chief guest. But sometimes one may sit beside another and all the while be thousands of miles away. Just as two may live in the same dwelling and sleep under the same roof at night, and yet seas between them "broad may roar." Many a young fellow is nearer Keats[2] or Shelley[3] than he is to the fellow-clerk on the next stool. Real nearness differs from proximity. And that night, though seated next to Simon, our Lord was really separate from Simon by a gulf it is impossible to measure. The One a provincial from Galilee, the other trained in the learning of the schools. The One with love filling His great heart, the other discourteous and cold and legal. And yet across that gulf the Savior reaches with His searching and revealing word—"Simon, I have somewhat to say unto thee." That is the wonder of the word of Christ. It is universal. It bridges every gulf. Men hear that word in their own tongue, as they did at the miracle of Pentecost. He has somewhat to say to the millions of India.

---

1. From "In the Valley of Cauteretz" by Tennyson.
2. John Keats (1795–1821), English poet.
3. Percy Bysshe Shelley (1792–1822), English poet.

He has somewhat to say to the myriads of China. He has somewhat to say to the New Guinea cannibals. When one thinks of our industrial civilization and compares it with the environment of Jesus, it might seem incredible that that lone Man of Galilee should have anything to say to *us*. Yet there come times when we most profoundly feel that there is no one who understands us and our problems like the Guest who was in Simon's house that night.

Then, too, we must not forget that our Lord has something *personal* to say. To his intense surprise Simon discovered that. I imagine that when he invited Christ to dinner, he was counting on some splendid talk. Had he not heard from the assembly officers that never man spoke like this man? Simon was a man who loved good talk and had an abhorrence of gossip at the dinner-table as every decent person ought to have. He would get this prophet to talk of the Old Testament—He was said to have strange views of the Old Testament. He would get Him to speak about the Coming One. He would urge Him to tell one of His beautiful stories. And then suddenly and in the deathlike silence came what he was never looking for: "Simon, I have somewhat to say *unto thee*." It was a word for him and him alone. It was intensely personal and individual. It reached his solitary, selfish heart. It probed his conscience and convicted him. And that is the abiding wonder of the Lord, that He speaks to each of us in such a way that there might be no one else in the wide world at all. He holds the answer to the vastest problems. He has a message for international relationships. But when we listen to Him, He never leaves us brooding on international relationships. As He speaks to me, I come to realize that the problem of all problems is myself. "Simon, I have somewhat to say *unto thee*."

"My joy" (John 15:11).

19

The Joy of the Lord

Our Lord, especially as the days advanced, frequently spoke about His joy, and the notable thing is that when He spoke so none of His disciples was surprised. Nobody ever asked Him what He meant. They did not look at each other in perplexity. To them it seemed entirely natural that the Master should make reference to His gladness. From which we gather that the joy of Christ was something they were perfectly familiar with, both in His radiant and lofty hours and in His periods of lowly duty. There is much that is quite dark to us unless His joy was an intense reality. There is the element of rejoicing in His teaching. There is the note of exultancy in the New Testament. There is the attitude of His Pharisaic enemies who, trained in the prophets, understood His sorrow but never could understand His joy.

It was not because He was a man of sorrows that the religious leaders looked askance at Him. It was because He was a man of joy, utterly different from John the Baptist. They were looking for a lone Messiah whose face would be marred more than any man's, and our Lord proclaimed Himself a *bridegroom.* His joy, then, was an intense reality even on the witness of His enemies. It is because He stands at the back of the New Testament that the New Testament is an exultant book. And it is a profoundly interesting ques-

tion, and a question which concerns us all, to try to discover some at
least of the sources of the joy of Christ.

One of the sources of His joy, for instance, was the fullness of
life which He possessed. It is remarkable how often that word
fullness is brought in as descriptive of the Lord. We all know how
when *physical* life is full, its concomitant and sacrament is joy. We
see that on every hand in nature; we see it in the healthy little child.
And when one thinks of the inner life of Christ and of the fullness
that characterized that inner life, one begins to understand His joy.
Morally He was in perfect poise with Heaven. Spiritually He had
the fullness of the Spirit. No slightest disobedience to the Highest
ever cast its shadow on His soul. And that fullness of His inward
life, like the fullness of physical life in nature, had its concomitant
and sacrament in joy. I am come, He said, that others might have
life and that they might have it *abundantly*. He came to give what
He Himself possessed. And that abundant life, rooted in His sinlessness and continually enriched by new obedience, was one of the
splendid secrets of His joy.

Another never-failing source was His abiding in His Father's
love. We see that very clearly in the verse which immediately pre-
cedes our text (John 15:10). From it we gather that the joy of Jesus
was rooted in the presence of the Father, realized every moment
that He lived. There is a well-known story of a Scots divine, how
once, walking on the grassy hills, he met a shepherd with a joyless
look and said to him, quietly, "Do you know the Father?" And
some years afterward, so the tale is told, when the minister had
forgotten all about it, the shepherd, with gladness in his face, came
up to him and said, "*I know the Father now, sir.*" That shepherd had
passed out of his isolation into the great fellowship of God. He had
moved out of all his worrying care into the calming certainty of
love. And in a vision of that love unparalleled, the Good Shepherd
lived and toiled and died, and that was one great secret of His joy.
To Him it was a shelter from the storm and a shadow from the heat
of life. It comforted His heart when men were mocking Him. It
sustained Him in the hour of agony. His joy was not only rooted in
His fullness, it was rooted in the love of Heaven which to *Him*,
every moment that He lived, was closer than breathing, nearer than
hands or feet.

And then we must not forget one other source: it was His entire surrender to vocation. Our Lord gave Himself in utter self-surrender to the task appointed Him of God. The first impression which the Gospels make on us is that of the freedom of the life of Jesus. He moves hither and thither in sweet liberty. Like the song of the thrush, His words are unpremeditated. And then we read more closely and discover that through all the various freedom of that life, like the beat of the screw in some great ocean liner, is the throb of a sovereign dominating purpose. "I come to do Thy will, O God. My meat is to do the will of Him that sent Me. I have a baptism to be baptized with, and how am I straitened until it be accomplished" (John 4:34). And that devotion, that utter self-surrender, that dedication to a high vocation was for *Him*, as it is for every man, one of the deep sources of His joy. Skimp in your work and you are never glad. Do it half-heartedly and glooms are everywhere. But give yourself to it with heart and soul and strength, and all the birds are singing on the trees. And it was just because our Lord so gave Himself to a vocation which led Him to the Cross, that "God, even His God, anointed Him with the oil of gladness above His fellows" (Heb. 1:9).

"In all points tempted like as we are" (Heb. 4:15).

20

The Temptations of Calvary

That our Lord's temptations were intensely real is the accepted faith of Christendom. He was tempted in all points like as we are. Unless He was really and cruelly tempted and knew the full meaning of resistance, He can never in any helpful way be the friend of tempted men and women. And if He is not Friend, then He is not Savior, for a Savior, whatever else he is, must be vitally identified with man. Our Lord's sinlessness was not endowment. It was rather an unparalleled achievement. It was not a gift bestowed on Him by heaven. It was a moral and spiritual victory. It was wrought out, moment after moment, by a will sustained in perfect poise with God, instantly and unswervingly obedient. Now always where the heart is there is the sorest onset of temptation. Temptation has always its eye upon the citadel, though it may seem to be leveled at the outworks. And that is why, right through the gospel story, the bitterest temptations of our Lord are to be found converging on the Cross. How, then, was our Lord tempted in regard to the great experience of Calvary? To what suggestions, winging from the darkness, had He to offer victorious resistance? Let us reverently give our thought to that.

We see Him first, and we see Him often, tempted *to avoid the Cross*. That sore temptation never left Him. At the very outset of His ministry, such was the suggestion of the devil. It runs like some dark thread of hell through all the encounters of the wilderness. Let Him with all His brilliant gifts ally Himself with worldly policies, and what need of the bloody way of Calvary? It smote Him again after many days, and this time through the lips of Simon Peter. Was not our Lord recalling the scene out in the wilderness when He said, "Get thee behind Me, *Satan*" (Matt. 16:23)? And near the end when the Greeks came craving an interview with Christ, was that not the old temptation back again? Why, in that thrilling hour, did our Lord say "Now is My soul *troubled*" (John 12:27)? Why did He not rejoice in spirit when the "other sheep" were coming to His feet? Surely it was because these Greeks were envoys, offering an open door to the big world without the imminent agonies of Calvary. It is notable that in the Gospel of St. John there is no mention whatever of Gethsemane. To St. John that offer of the Grecian world was the spiritual equivalent of Gethsemane. It was the temptation to achieve the kingship on which His kingly heart was set by some way other than the Cross. He was tempted to avoid the Cross, to shun it, to take some other road. Have we not all been tempted just like that? And does it not bring the Master very near us in a brotherhood intensely real, to remember that He was victorious just there?

Once again our Savior was tempted *to hasten on the Cross.* He was tempted to antedate the hour of God. We read, for instance, that when the sisters sent for Him, He abode two days still in the same place where He was (John 11:6). For one who was the Good Pysician, that was an extraordinary thing to do. If *we* summoned our doctor to a dear one and if for two days he never came, we should find it very hard to call him good. Was He waiting to augment the miracle? But then Lazarus was already dead (11:39). Was He waiting to test the sisters' faith? But is *that* how Jesus deals with loving friends? He was waiting because He saw so clearly that the raising of Lazarus would seal His doom (11:53), and He dreaded to antedate the hour of God. Human love was calling Him to Bethany. Affection for His friends was calling Him. Going, He signed His death-warrant—but was it His Father's *will* that He should die yet?

And so, though drawn by the cords of love to go, He waited in quiet fellowship with Heaven until the will of God was perfectly revealed. How often had He said, "Mine hour is not yet come." With what profound conviction did He know that God had His appointed hour for Calvary. Might not these drawings of love be but the devil's stratagem to interfere with the ordered times of heaven?—and He abode two days still in the same place where He was. Once more does that not bring Him very near us? Have we not all been tempted to hurry on God's hour? There are few things more difficult in life, sometimes, than just to wait patiently for God. And *He* was tempted in all points like as we are.

Lastly our Lord was tempted *to come down from the Cross.* "Let Him come down from the Cross and we will believe Him" (Matt. 27:42). When these voices broke upon His ear, were they not fraught with terrible temptation? Think of the agony He was enduring in His so sensitive and sinless frame. Think how the very passion of His heart was that these men and women should believe in Him. And as these cries rang upon His ear, did they not carry with them the suggestion that in one instant He might escape His torture and, doing it, win the allegiance of His own? Tempted in every prospect of the Cross, our Lord was tempted on the Cross itself. By one swift action might He not end His agony and win the great ambition of His life? And the wonderful thing is that on the Cross, as in the desert at the opening of His ministry, He steeled Himself against these tempting voices. *They* said, "Come down, and we will believe in you" (Matt. 27:40). *We* believe because He did not come down. To us the glory is in His hanging there, until He cried in a loud voice, "It is finished" (John 19:30). And when *we* are tempted, as we so often are, to release ourselves when "crucified with Christ," what a comfort that we can quietly say, "He was tempted in all points like as we are."

"Consider the lilies of the field" (Matt. 6:28).

21

Our Lord and Nature

Our Lord, the lover of mankind, was a lover also of the world of nature. It called Him, and calling spoke to Him; it was His inspiration and His rest. When you love a person you never can quite hide it. There are some secrets nobody can hide. You say I shall never mention the beloved, but the birds of the air are carrying the tidings. So in the Gospels, given for our redemption, one is never far away from nature, just because the Master loved it so. He loved Peter, and you see Peter there. He loved John, and John is in the picture. But He also loved the sparrows and the lilies and the wind that blows where it will—and the Gospels have to give house-room to them all.

No doubt the Master's love of nature sprang in part from the setting of His birth. The world is always vocal to the Hebrew, and our Lord was born of Hebrew lineage. It is a curious thing that the word *Jew* carries for us the suggestion of the city. We picture the Jew in the markets of the world and not against the background of its greenness. But as a matter of historic fact, the Jew was the nature-lover of antiquity, far more responsive than the Roman and with a deeper vision than the Greek. You can often tell what a nation gives its heart to by the relative wealth of its vocabulary, and in nothing is the Hebrew language richer than in its vocabulary of the open world. It has two or three different words for sun and moon, two or three different words for grass and corn, ten words descriptive of the rain. Into that heritage our Savior entered. He was born of a race that brooded on the world. He was the son of Abraham, who watched the stars and of Isaac, who meditated in the fields at eventide. And if the glory of nature shines on the Gospel page, we owe it in part to the ordering of heaven which sent the Son into a Hebrew home.

Yet when you study the Old Testament and then turn to the teaching of our Lord, what arrests is not the similarity, rather it is the sense of contrast. To psalmist and prophet (excepting Jeremiah), nature is generally terrible. It is a mighty pageant of mysterious forces striking awe into the human breast. And the notable thing is that when you come to Jesus, who was reared on these very prophecies and psalms, immediately you breathe a different air. You see the lilies in their summer beauty and the birds nesting in the trees. You see the weed growing beside the highway and the sparrows chirping in the eaves. You see the hen calling her little innocents to the soft and downy shelter of her breast. You see the sower going forth to sow. It is a kindlier and a gentler world. There is a homelike touch about it all. The mystery of fear seems to have vanished, and the greater mystery of love has come. What, then, is the secret of that change?

May I suggest that you never can explain it by the earthly experience of our Lord. Had Jesus had a kindly lot, His kindly world would have been natural. It is natural to find around us the transcript of our own experience. If we are happy all the world is happy; if our hearts are tuneful all the world is musical. But our Savior was a man of sorrows, and He drank the cup of suffering to the dregs, and cruel hands nailed Him to the tree. Not for Him the companionships of home nor the loving appreciation of "His own." He was spat upon and put to open shame. His face was marred more than any man's. And the amazing thing is that through a life like that, bearing the sin and sorrow of the world, He saw the lilies and heard the wind whispering and had an open eye even for the sparrows. Burns said: "Thou'lt break my heart, thou warbling bird, that wantons thro' the flowering thorn."[1] But it was not the birds

---

1. From "The Banks o' Doun," by Robert Burns (1759-1796).

that broke the heart of Jesus. It was the sin of man. For Him, with all the weight of the world's sorrow, nature was genial, intimate, and kindly, and it was so right on to the end.

Now surely the secret of it all is this, that our Savior found His Father in the world. He did not grope for Him as you and I must do. Vividly and universally He found Him. Christ was not blind to the terrible in nature. He saw it as clearly as the prophets did. He saw the vultures gathering to the carrion and the floods that could sweep a house away. But everywhere in vivid, intense intimacy was the sense and feeling of His Father and, with it, the kindliness of home. Twelve times over in this chapter He speaks of the Creator as the Father. The Father's hand controlled the lightning just as truly as it clothed the lilies. It was *that* assurance, flooding the heart of Jesus, that made all nature what it was to Him. Perfect love had come and cast out fear.

"Take My yoke upon you, and learn of Me: . . . and ye shall find rest unto your souls" (Matt. 11:29).

22

His Yoke

There are, I think, three thoughts that meet and mingle in this beautiful figure of the yoke. The first is the great thought of *surrender*. When the Romans conquered some rebellious tribe, they made the vanquished pass under the yoke. It thus became a figure of common speech that the conquered were under the yoke of the victorious. And our Lord, who had seen the legions marching and who was quite familiar with the figure, says, "Take My yoke upon you." Nothing is more magnificent in Christ than the way in which He demands a full surrender. He does not claim a little bit of life. He claims life in its wholeness and entirety. And the strange thing is that whenever that is yielded and never until that is yielded, the life is flooded with the sense of rest. Such a surrender to anybody else would mean the warping of the personality. But *that* it never means with Christ. It means the liberation of the personality. No man is ever really himself until he has fully surrendered to the Lord. Take My yoke upon you—and find rest.

This, you observe, is not a *forced* surrender. Our Lord says, *Take* My yoke upon you. Our Lord is very fond of the word *must*, but He never uses it in this connection. When the Roman legions smashed some savage tribe, that tribe were compelled to bear the yoke. Often, on that account, they hated Rome and served her with rebellion in their hearts. But Christ wants nobody on terms like these. Such terms are not in the program of His conquest. Christ demands a surrender that is willing. You can compel the dog to do your bidding. You can force the slave to carry out your will. But Christ, that mighty protagonist of liberty, treats nobody as a dog or as a slave. We are the Father's children, made in the Father's image with an inalienable heritage of freedom, and we may take or we may spurn the yoke. There are so many who are waiting for something irresistible to happen, something to sweep them off their feet to Christ as the breaker sweeps the log on to the shore. *That something is never going to happen.* Now is the accepted time. The Master's word is, "*Take* My yoke upon you."

The next suggestion of our text is that of *service*, for the yoke at once suggests the thought of service. Our Lord had coupled the two thoughts a hundred times as He wandered among the farms of Galilee. I love to watch the horses on a farm when the evening hour of their unyoking comes—the big, beautiful creatures free at last from the toiling and the straining of the day. So they pass to the water-trough and to the stalls, until with the morning the yoke is on again: the yoke, the symbol and sacrament of service. Now all life is service, and perhaps "all service ranks the same with God," from that of the starveling in Sally Brass's[1] kitchen to that of the Prime Minister of Britain. And then Christ comes to all who have to serve, no matter how high or how low their service is, and says, "Take *My* yoke upon you, and find rest." It is not of rest *from* service that He speaks. It is of rest *in* service. It is of rest that comes when care and worry vanish and the burden no longer irritates and frets. For duty is different now, and God is near, and love is everywhere, and strength sufficient when once the yoke of Christ is on the shoulders.

That our Lord had full authority for speaking so is evident to every student of His life. *He* served with an intensity unparalleled, yet who would ever think to call Him restless? Busy and broken were His days, yet He had the heart at leisure from itself. The crowds thronged Him and the calls were overwhelming, yet He

---

1. The villanous sister of Sampson Brass in *Old Curiousity Shop* by Charles Dickens.

moved in the peace that passes understanding. And now He says, "Take *My* yoke upon you. It is My passion to pass on My secret. Take My yoke upon you—and find rest." When a man flings himself into his toil without one word of prayer or thought of God, can you wonder if his nerves get jangled or if he is tempted now and then to give things up? But we are not here to give things up if the ordering of God is a reality. We are here just to give up *ourselves*. To take Christ's yoke upon us is to serve in the spirit that made all His service beautiful, with the same unfaltering trust that God was over Him and that the everlasting arms were underneath Him. *That* gave Him peace when burdens grew intolerable. Sustained by *that*, He never gave things up. He gave *Himself* up upon the Cross.

And then our text suggests another thought. It is the infinite comfort of *society*. The yoke is a double yoke (as Matthew Henry[2] said), and *we* are going to draw along with *Him*. Farmers tell me they sometimes train a young beast by yoking it with an old experienced beast, one that is familiar with the plow and has been out on many a raw and stormy morning. And Christ says, "I want you to pull with Me, and then you will learn to make a straighter furrow, and the farmer will be well contented in the evening." He has been over all the ground before. He knows it well and all its inequalities. He has been tempted in all points like as we are (Heb. 4:15). He has borne the heat and burden of the day. And then He comes to us, worrying and anxious and wondering how we shall ever carry on, and He says, *"Child, let's do this thing together."* It is the offer of partnership with God in the strain and stress of unillumined days. The question is, Have we accepted it? Is it a great reality to us? If not, why not accept it *now*?

---

2. Matthew Henry (1662–1714), English Non-conformist pastor and Bible commentator.

"Every man heard them speak in his own language" (Acts 2:6).

23

The Pentecostal Blessing

Let us reverently try to understand what happened on that day of Pentecost. It is rightly called the birthday of the Church. Ten days before, the Savior had ascended. He had passed into the presence of the Father. He had left His little band of faithful followers to be witnesses for Him. And yet the strange thing is that though they trusted Him and were perfectly convinced that He was risen, they were not ready yet to be His witness-bearers. All of them believed in Jesus, but for witness-bearing something more was needed: some new power and fullness in their lives that would carry conviction to the world. And *that* is what the disciples got at Pentecost—that new power and fullness of the Spirit which changed them from convinced believers into equipped witnesses for Christ. Without it they would have returned to Galilee, "the world forgetting, and by the world forgot."[1] Without it, in daily fellowship with Christ, they would quietly have lived and died. With it there was a spiritual power about them that was mightier than any argument. They were witness-bearers to the living Christ. The Pentecostal blessing was equipment. It was adequacy for vocation. It was endowment for the stupendous task of the evangelization of the world. And of all this

---

1. From "Epigram" by Alexander Pope (1688–1744).

the sound as of the wind and the appearance as of tongues of fire were but the vivid and evanescent symbols.

We may illustrate the day of Pentecost from the experience of the Lord Himself. He, too, born of the Holy Spirit, had to tarry for power from on high. For thirty years He lived at Nazareth. It was a life of the most perfect beauty. In every thought, in every word and deed, He was inspired and guided by the Spirit. And yet these years, so spiritually beautiful, were for the Redeemer waiting years. He was tarrying for power from on high. *That* was given at His baptism when the Holy Spirit descended like a dove. Then was He endowed with power from God for His stupendous vocation of redemption. And like that moment in the life of Jesus when the fullness of the equipping Spirit rested on Him was Pentecost to the earliest disciples. It was not the hour when they were born again. They were saved followers long before that morning. They would have won their crown and had their welcome though the day of Pentecost had never dawned. Pentecost was power for witness-bearing. It was equipment for vocation. It was the needed and adequate endowment for the evangelizing of the world.

It is thus we see the very deep significance of the first expression of that adequacy. They began to speak, we read, with other tongues as the Spirit gave them utterance. Parthians, Medes, and Elamites were there—people from every country under heaven, of different languages and diverse cultures, separate as the East is from the West. And the first glorious effect of Pentecost was to make every man and woman know that here was something sent of Heaven for *them*. Somehow, through the power of God, they were listening to familiar accents. The message was for *them*; they understood it; it broke its way through every racial barrier. Avenues were opened, ways were cleared, entrances were instantly discovered to hearts which before Pentecost were sealed. Later on, in the letters of St. Paul, we read about another gift of tongues. I want you very carefully to notice that that was different from this of Pentecost. *That* was impassioned and ecstatic utterance which was unintelligible save for an interpreter; *this* was speaking to be understood. No need at Pentecost for an interpreter. The Holy Spirit Himself was the interpreter. He gathered an audience out of every country to typify the universal heart. And then He so inspired those earliest witnesses that everybody who heard them understood and felt that the message was for them.

Now I take it that in its literal form that miracle will never be repeated. I never heard of any foreign missionary receiving by sudden gift a foreign language. Yet I profoundly feel that whenever to the Church there comes a time of Pentecostal blessing, this evidence is manifestly present. Take an inspired man like Mr. Spurgeon.[2] Think of the crowds in Mr. Spurgeon's tabernacle. What an infinitely varied audience drawn from every section of society. The rich and poor, the gentleman and beggar, the saint and the poor wastrel from the street—and yet everybody heard in his own tongue. Filled with the Holy Spirit, he spoke his message, and God in His infinite wisdom did the rest, touching the message with some familiar chords for lives that were as separate as the poles. And whenever there comes to the Church a time of Pentecost, *that* is one seal of its appointed ministry—everybody hears in his own tongue. Men do not say, "I cannot understand. The preacher's tongue is alien from mine." The witness-bearing breaks through every barrier, and deep begins calling unto deep. Clothed with grace, the universal gospel is spoken in a universal language—not by might nor by power, but by *My Spirit*, says the Lord (Zech. 4:6).

---

2. Charles H. Spurgeon (1834–1892), influential English Baptist preacher.

"Approving ourselves . . . in necessities"
(2 Cor. 6:4).

24

The Unescapable Elements of Life

When the apostle speaks about necessities he does not think of
necessary things. That is not the sense of the original. There *are*
things, the opposite of luxuries, without which we could not live at
all. Such are food and drink, and the air of heaven to breathe, and
the refreshing ministry of sleep. But "necessities," in the idiom of
the Greek, does not connote such necessary things; it means experiences from which there is no escape. It is in such experiences Paul
wants to be approved—to show himself the gallant Christian gentleman. He is determined to reveal his faith and joy in the unescapable elements of life. And so, brooding upon the text, one comes to
ask the question, what are those things no one can escape from in
the strange and intricate complex of experience?

One thinks first of certain bitter things that reach men in the
realm of mind or body. There are sufferings which pass away; there
are others out of which is no escape. If a man falls ill of diphtheria
or fever, he recovers in the good providence of God. If he meets
with an accident and breaks his arm, that fracture may be perfectly
united. But there are other things in the range of human ills from

which there is no prospect of escape in the long vista of the coming years. There is blindness; there is lameness; there is deafness; there is congenital deformity of body. There are brains that never can be brilliant and faces that never can be beautiful. There are thorns in the flesh, messengers of Satan hindering influence and power and service, that are going to be present to the end. It is in things like these that Paul is quite determined to show himself an approved minister of God—brave and bright, faithful to his task, free from the slightest trace of jaundiced bitterness. And to do *that* is a far higher thing than to come untarnished from temporary trial. It is to "come smiling from the world's great snare, uncaught."[1]

Then one's thoughts go winging to temptation, for temptation is one of the "necessities" of life. Separate from each other in a thousand ways, we are all united in temptation. A man may escape the gnawing tooth of poverty or the anguish and the languor of disease. He may escape imprisonments and stripes and the "slings and arrows of outrageous fortune."[2] But no man, be he wise or simple, rich as Croesus[3] or poor as Bartimæus,[4] ever escapes the onset of temptation. Temptation is a most obsequious servant. It follows a man everywhere, into the church, into the sheltered study, into the sweetest and tenderest relationships. Men fly to the desert to escape temptation only to find that it is there before them, insistent as in the crowded haunts of men. *That* is the reason why our Lord was tempted. A Christ untempted would be no Christ for me. He might be the Son of God in all His fullness, but He never for me could be the Son of Man. It is in such "necessities," or in our Western idiom, such unescapable elements of life, that the apostle yearns in Christ, to play the man. Is there any finer victory than that? To resist the devil when he leaps or creeps on us, clad in the most alluring of disguises; to do it not once, but steadily and doggedly, for when the devil comes he always comes again—*that* is a far higher thing than to pass untouched from temporary trial. It is to stand (as Browning says) pedestalled in triumph.[5]

Another of the "necessities" of life is what our Savior calls the cross. Just as in every lot there is a crook, so in every life there is a cross. You

---

1. From *Antony and Cleopatra* by Shakespeare.
2. From *Hamlet* by Shakespeare.
3. Croesus, king of Lydia (560–546 B.C.), legendary for great wealth.
4. Mark 10:46, blind beggar of Jericho.
5. From "La Saisiaz" by Robert Browning.

remember how our Lord declared this—"If *any man* will come after Me, let him take up his cross" (Luke 9:23)—*not* certain men in strange peculiar circumstances, but *any man*, right to the end of time. From which we gather that in the eyes of Christ the cross was universal in experience, one of the things that nobody escapes. The cross is anything very hard to carry—anything that takes liberty from living—anything that robs the foot of fleetness or silences the music of the heart. And men may be brave and hide the cross away and wreathe it with flowers so that none suspects it, but, says Jesus, it is always there. There are only two things men can do with crosses—they can take them up or they can kick against them. They can merge them in God's plan of life for them, or they can stumble over them toward the glen of weeping. And what could be finer in the whole range of life than just to determine, as the apostle did, to be divinely approved in the cross? To take the cross up every November morning and to do it happily for Jesus' sake—never to quarrel with God for its intrusion—never to lose heart nor faith nor love—that fine handling of one of life's "necessities" is indispensable to following Christ and is, through Him, in the compass of us all.

One last "necessity" remains: it is the grim necessity of death. For sooner or later death comes to every man; from the grip of death nobody escapes. Men used to ponder deeply upon death. Philosophy was the preparation for it. Books were written that dealt with holy dying. Preachers preached "as dying men to dying men."[6] Now that has passed—men's thoughts are turned to life—they have abandoned the contemplation of the grave; and yet from death nobody escapes. Death is the last and grimmest of "necessities." "The paths of glory lead but to the grave."[7] Death, like temptation and the cross, is an unescapable element of life. And then the apostle says: "In that last hour, when my eyes close on the familiar faces, God grant me grace to show myself approved." I go to be with Christ which is far better (Phil. 1:23). O Death, where is thy sting? (1 Cor. 15:55). The Lord God is merciful and gracious, blotting out our transgressions like a cloud. With such a hope, with such a Father-God, with such a Savior on the other shore, the very weakest need not fear to die.

---

6. Richard Baxter (1615–1619), English Puritan minister and writer. From *Love Breathing Thanks and Praise*:
   "I preach as never sure to preach again,
   And as a dying man to dying men."
7. From "Elegy in a Country Churchyard" by Thomas Gray (1716-1771).

"There was a man in the synagogue which had a withered hand" (Mark 3:1).

25

The Kind of Man He Was

If we center our attention on this man, we see him as a quite ordinary person. He was one of the crowd of undistinguished people who go to church upon the Sabbath-day. Tradition says he was a bricklayer, and quite probably that is true. It at least indicates the old belief that this was a quite ordinary person. And one of the striking things about the gospel is its perennial and amazing power over ordinary people like this bricklayer. He is not like Lazarus[1] or even Bartimæus[2] whose names have come ringing down the aisles of time. The only name his fellow-worshipers had for him was "the man with the withered hand." And that, from the first, is just the kind of man whom the gospel has been powerful to handle and to give back to usefulness again. That is what makes it a universal gospel—that heavenly power over nameless people. If lack of culture made it ineffectual, it could never be preached across the world. And the very fact that it *is* so preached, and preached with signs and wonders following, proclaims it as of the *Son of Man*.

---

1. Luke 16:20–25
2. Mark 10:46

Again we recognize him as a person who had had a hard and embittering experience. We feel the force of that more vividly when we turn to the Gospel of St. Luke. One of the charming things about Luke's Gospel is his illuminative touches in the miracles. Luke was a doctor with a doctor's eye, quick to observe everything pathological. He tells us that the leper was "full of leprosy" (Luke 5:12) and that Peter's mother-in-law was down with "a great fever" (Luke 4:38); here he reveals that the hand was the *right* hand. Nor, mark you, had the man been so from birth. This cruel affliction had come upon him gradually. His hand grew stiff; he lost the power of it; gradually it shrank and atrophied. Until now, when people passed him in the street, they glanced at him with commiseration and called him "the man with the withered hand." One thinks of everything that must have meant in a day when there were no insurances nor doles. His work gone—his children without bread—his wife a brokenhearted woman. It was a cruel thing—to all appearance meaningless, one of the taunting ironies of heaven—the years had brought him when he was never dreaming of it, a hard and most embittering experience. Such people are always a great company. There will be not a few of them among my readers. Nothing is so hard to bear in life as bitter things that seem devoid of meaning. And the beautiful thing is that it was just that kind of person whom our blessed Savior singled out that day in a synagogue which would be crowded.

And then, equally evident is this, that this man had not lost his faith; for first of all the Savior healed him, and faith is indispensable to miracle. Mark you, faith is not always *mentioned* in the miracles, nor is there any reason why it should be. It seems to me that faith, like beauty, is often in the eye of the beholder. Had you asked this man if he had faith, he might probably have answered in the negative, but Christ saw more in him than the man dreamed. I want to say a very comforting thing out of a long pastoral experience. I think that many people have more faith than they are ever willing to admit. Life is compact of faith; we could not live without it; we walk by faith through every common day—but it has never been turned upon the Lord. That is why Christ did not *ask* if he had faith. The man would probably have answered, "No." But Christ knew him, and read his inmost heart, and saw there what the man had never seen. That is why often the Lord can work so wonderfully and perform His miracles of grace on folk who lament they have no faith at all.

And then this man had not given up the church; that also is a witness to his faith. After his hard and embittering experience he was in the synagogue on that Sabbath-day. One can picture him in the old, happy days coming to church with his wife and children for life was pleasant then, and God was good to him, and there was work and bread upon his table. But *now*, impoverished—dependent upon others—with hungry children and a despairing wife—could you have wondered if he had stayed away? "The Lord is my shepherd, and I shall not want" (Ps. 23:1)—and his wife and children *were* in want. "The Lord God, merciful and gracious" (Ps. 103:8)—had He been merciful and gracious unto him? Quite evidently this was a great big soul, still simply trusting in the God of Jacob, and *that* the Lord instantly recognized. After that cruel irony of heaven, after that seemingly meaningless catastrophe, there he was in his familiar place, listening to the gracious news of heaven. What need to ask him, "Hast thou faith?" That sweet and simple continuance declared it—and, "being in the way," he won his crown.

But I keep the best wine to the last, for there is one thing more to be said about this bricklayer. He was a man who found that he could do what up to that hour he had deemed impossible. Do you not think his wife had often said to him, "Husband, try to stretch your hand this morning"? And he, feeling a little better perhaps, had tried, and always tried in vain. The delightful thing is that when the Lord commanded, somehow or other it was not in vain; the Lord said, "Stretch it out," and he just did it. He did not pray about it, nor discuss it, nor plead that it was utterly impossible. To his own intense amazement he just did it, though I daresay he could never tell you *how* he did it. But we, who know the mind of Christ far more intimately than the despairing bricklayer, are cognizant of the secret of the Lord. There may be seeming ironies in life; there are none in the commands of Christ. When He enjoins, He enables. When He commands, He gives the power. Despondent, on the margins of despair, with an enfeebled will or withered heart, *I can do all things through Christ who strengtheneth me* (Phil. 4:13).

"I wait on Thee" (Ps. 25:21).

26
Waiting Upon God

In the great Biblical thought of waiting upon God there are several interwoven strands of meaning. I propose to try to distinguish some of these that we may better grasp the import of the term. And first, nestling at the heart of it and never absent from the mind of any writer, is the large conception of *dependence*. As the little child waits upon its mother for without its mother it will die, as the anguished patient waits upon the surgeon for in the skill of the surgeon is the hope of life, so when one is said to wait on God there is implied an entire dependence upon Him. There is a sense in Biblical phraseology in which this waiting is a universal thing. "The eyes of all things living wait on Thee" (Ps. 145:15). The bird that sings, the beast that hunts its prey—all of them are waiting upon God. But such an unescapable dependence does not bring the thought to its full blossoming. *That* demands a dependence which is conscious. It is when we realize, however dimly, that in Him we live and move and have our being (Acts 17:28), it is when we waken to the mysterious certainty that we all hang on God for every heartbeat—it is only then the word comes to its fullness in the deep usage of the Scriptures, and man is said to be waiting upon God.

Another strand of meaning in the word takes us into the region of *obedience*. "To wait on," is another term for service. The man who

serves us when we sit at table and who is there just to supply our
wants, we still distinguish by the name of *waiter*. When the Prime
Minister waits upon the King, that is not an idle sauntering business. It is part of the service to which he has been called, a service
which demands his highest energies. And so when a man is said to
wait on God, that is not a negation of activity, for the thought of
service runs right through the term. We wait on God whenever we
help a friend and do it lovingly for Jesus' sake. We wait on God
when we teach our little class or climb the stair to cheer some
lonely soul. The servant in the kitchen waits on God when for His
sake she does her duty faithfully. The mistress in the drawing-room
waits on God when for His sake she is a lady to her servants. We
are all apt to forget that and to narrow down these fine old Bible
words. We are prone to limit the great thought of waiting to the
single region of devotion. But the root idea of it is not devotion. The
root idea is simple, quiet obedience. And what does the Lord our
God require of you but to obey?

Another of the interwoven strands is *love*; in true waiting that is
invariably present. As love is the source of all the highest work, so
is it the spring of all the finest waiting. Jacob waited for Rachel
seven years, and the years were as a day or two to Jacob because
of the great love he bare her (Gen. 29). What makes the mother
wait upon her child and start from her pillow when she hears it
cry? What makes her wait on it with tireless patience when it frets
or tosses in some childish fever? She may be only a frail and
sickly woman, but she never wearies of waiting on her child, and
the secret of it is a mother's love. Love bears all things and
endures all things (1 Cor. 13:7). Love can wait with a patience all
her own. Love can achieve miracles of waiting, as many a young
affianced couple knows. And *that* is why, if we are ever to wait
nobly in the teeth of all our natural impatience, we must be taught
to love the Lord our God. It must have been very hard in the times
of the older covenant for the common man to wait on God. For
God seemed very far away then, and clouds and darkness were
about His throne. But now, under the new covenant and by the
revealing grace of the Redeemer, it is within the reach and compass of us all. If we hold to it that "God so loved the world" (John
3:16), if we say believingly "Our Father," love to God, once so
supremely difficult, is in the range of the ordinary heart. And,

lovingly, we can wait as Jacob waited and as the mother waits upon her child with a service that knows no weariness at all.

There is one other strand woven in the word, and that is the strand of eager, tense *expectancy*. To wait on in a hundred spheres of life is eagerly and tensely to expect. You see that in the dumb creatures—watch the dog waiting on his master. Is the master going to give him a bit of food? Is he going to throw that stick into the stream? You see that in any court of law when the accused waits on the verdict of the judge with an expectancy so tense that it is pain. Now apply that to the realm of prayer and how it illuminates the matter! To wait on God is not just to pray to God, for many pray and never expect an answer. To wait on God is to pray with tense expectancy that the prayer we offer will be answered, for He is the answerer of prayer. All prayer is *not* waiting upon God in the full and lofty sense of the Old Testament. For a man may rise from his knees and forget the thing he prayed for and fail to keep on the outlook for an answer. Only when we pray and pray believingly and climb the watch-tower to see the answer coming, do we reach the fullness of that fine old word *waiting upon God.*

" . . . whatever ye shall ask in prayer,
believing, ye shall receive" (Matt. 21:22).

27

Prayers That Are Refused

One of the problems of the spiritual life is the problem of unanswered prayer. It is one of the earliest problems to emerge, and it
lingers among the memories of childhood. Dr. Horton[1] tells that
when he was a child he was faced by a perplexity like this. He had a
farthing in a certain drawer and he prayed that God would turn it
into gold. And when he opened the drawer after the act of prayer
and discovered that the coin was still a farthing, it was very staggering to his faith. At such things we are prone to smile, but to children
they are intensely real. They shake the pillars of their childish universe and often cast a shadow upon God. It grows more difficult to
pray for things in all the sweet simplicity of faith when God has
been clearly powerless with a farthing. There are childish problems
which vanish with the years, but that of prayer unanswered never
vanishes. Sooner or later it comes back again, most often in the life
of intercession. And that is why in the story of the Gospel, written
for our spiritual help and comforting, we have instances of prayers
that were refused.

There is, for example, the Gadarene demoniac who prayed that

---

1. Thomas Horton (d. 1673), English clergyman.

he might company with Jesus (Mark 5:18–19). One might be certain *that* prayer would be granted by Him who used to say "Come unto Me." It was a prayer that sprang from an adoring gratitude, for the Lord had changed him to a man again. It was a prayer that was born of conscious weakness; he dreaded the thought of being left alone. And yet that prayer, wrung from a grateful heart which felt there was only safety in the Presence, was quietly and deliberately refused. The devils prayed for entrance to the swine, and that was granted them immediately. The citizens prayed that Jesus would depart, and He bade the disciples hoist the sail and go. The only prayer which was refused that day, when the Lord was clearly in a granting spirit, was the prayer of the Gadarene demoniac. To him it must have seemed inexplicable. It was a crushing and staggering refusal. It was as if the Lord were done with him when He could bar him from His presence so. But to *us*, surveying the whole scene, things are no longer mysterious and dark; they are luminous with wisdom and with mercy. What use would the man have been across the lake? Were the children of Abraham to be taught by aliens? Nobody knew him there, and none had seen him when he was in the horrid grip of Legion. But at home everybody knew him; they had talked about him at a hundred hearths, they had heard his cry come ringing through the night. His prayer was *not* refused because Christ spurned him. It was refused in the interests of service. The man could do far finer things at home than by traveling to a foreign shore. And when prayers for larger service are refused and every door is barred save the home-door, it is well to remember the Gadarene demoniac.

Another instance is that of the apostle Paul when he prayed that God would take away his thorn (2 Cor. 12:7–10). How passionately he prayed for that we shall never know until we meet him. It was not for his own ease that he was praying. He was not beseeching to be freed from pain. He rejoiced to share in the sufferings of his Lord whose head had once been crowned with thorns on Calvary. What made him pray so eagerly and passionately that the sharp and festering thorn might be removed was its interference with his appointed service. What he would do if only that were gone! What new strength would be added to his voice! What a new appeal he would make to the Greek world, for the Greeks loved strength and beauty in a man. And then, in the highest interests of that service which the apostle thought his thorn in the flesh was hindering, his eager prayer was steadily refused. That very hindrance was a means of grace. It cast him, body and spirit, on the Lord. It made men feel, when the word came home with power, that the power was not human but divine. So once again in the unanswered prayer there was vision and love and wisdom far more wonderful than any immediate answer would have shown.

Then, lastly, there is the prayer of Jesus, "If it be possible let this cup pass from Me" (Matt. 26:39). Like the apostle, He prayed that prayer three times in the last and sorest conflict of Gethsemane. There was more in that prayer than shrinking of the flesh. There was more in that bitter cup than human suffering. What made the drinking of that cup so awful was that it was red with human sin. And God so loved the world and was so gloriously bent on its redemption, that that great cry of His own Well-beloved was (with an infinite suffering) refused. Had it been granted, there had been no Calvary and no glad cry on Calvary, "It is finished" (John 19:30). Had it been granted, no one had ever sung, "When I survey the wondrous Cross."[2] Had it been granted no poor despairing soul could ever have quietly said, "He died for me," and so believing, found himself at peace. Do you not think God yearned to grant that prayer just as He yearns to grant your prayer and mine? Was He not afflicted in His Son's affliction, being a Father with a father's heart? I trust I am not irreverent in thinking that today in glory the Savior thanks His Father that that thrice-repeated petition was refused. When we reach home, we shall see far more clearly than we ever see in this dark and cloudy world. We shall be thankful for a thousand things that here we utterly fail to understand. I sometimes think that blended with our gratitude for all the goodness and mercy that have followed us will be a great thankfulness (knowing as we are known) for all our prayers down here that were refused.

---

2. By Isaac Watts (1674–1748), English hymn writer.

"God commendeth His love toward us, in that, while we were yet sinners, Christ died for us" (Rom. 5:8).

28

Love's Argument

The word commend is a much stronger word than might appear to the casual reader. It means far more than to recommend. It means to exhibit, to demonstrate, to prove. There are certain attributes of God which do not call for any special proof. They are universally and luminously evident if it be granted there is a God at all. Nobody asks for any special proof, for instance, that God has an arm which is full of power or that He claims wisdom as His own. Now many imagine that the love of God is similar to His power or His wisdom. They picture it as something lumious, written large on the working of His hands. And one thing we must all learn, if our faith is to be equal to the stress of things, is that this *never* is the Bible standpoint. The love of God is not self-evident, according to the teaching of the Scripture. It is not manifest as His power is manifest nor written on the nightly heavens like His wisdom. On the contrary, if it is a fact, it is one against which a thousand facts seem ranged, and some overwhelming argument is needed to put these militating facts to flight.

Think, for a moment, of some of the many things which seem to tell against the love of God. One is, for instance, the struggle for existence that is ceaselessly waged among all living creatures. Man fights with man and beast with beast and bird with bird and fish with fish. To the seeing eye all nature is a battlefield, and its children are fighting for their life. That is why Huxley[1] wrote to Kingsley[2] once, in a great discussion they were having, that he found no proof in nature of what is called the fatherhood of God. Then there are the facts of our experience, often so difficult to reconcile with love, the things that come to men who are God's children which we should never dream of doing to *our* children. Providence is hard to understand, as when the chair is empty and the grave is full, and the one taken so desperately needed. How many have cried and are crying this very hour, how can God love me when He so deals with me? Armenian refugees[3] are crying that, and many a lonely broken heart at home here. And it is such things, things which seem so harsh, that call for special and tremendous proof for the doctrine that love is on the throne.

Now the wonderful thing about the Bible is that this proof is given in its pages. The Bible is a book for thoughtful people. It never takes the lovely summer day and says, "Behold your proof that God is love." It knows that before the beautiful day is ended there may be an awful earthquake in Japan. It never turns to the child in the mother's arms, saying, "Mother, behold your proof that God is love." It knows that before another year is gone that little child may be sleeping in its coffin. The Bible turns to the Cross of the Lord Jesus and finds *there* its unanswerable argument—"God demonstrateth His love toward us, in that while we were yet sinners Christ died for us." Once we have really understood the Cross, once we have grasped its inward spiritual meaning, there is one thing we can never do again—we can never again doubt the love of God. Whatever happens to us, whatever sorrows come, whatever trials that there is no explaining, the magnificent proof of Calvary remains.

Two things have to be said about this argument, and the first is that it is a *fact*. When you and I suspect that we are hated, a word is hardly enough to bring assurance. We want some unmistakably

---

1. T. H. Huxley (1825–1895), English biologist and writer.
2. Charles Kingsley (1819–1875), English clergyman, novelist and poet.
3. This sermon was preached during the World War I.

loving *deed* if our hearts are ever to rest in love again. And God, knowing that it is bitter facts which often tempt us to deny His love, gives us for our proof the fact of Calvary. I read the promises in the old prophets, or the glowing words of the Bridegroom in the Song,[4] and all the time my doubting heart keeps whispering that I am only listening to words. But the Cross of Christ is not a word spoken in some impassioned moment; it is a glorious and stupendous fact. No mere words could ever prove to us what so many facts of life seem to deny. But God does not ask us to rest our faith on words. He gives us as our argument for love the most tremendous fact in the world's history.

And then this argument is an *abiding* argument. God commends—forever. The apostle does not employ the past tense; he uses what we call the timeless present. There are proofs for the being and attributes of God which serve their purpose and then pass away. Powerful for one generation, they are not infrequently powerless for the next. But the Scripture argument for the love of God is an argument that can never pass away, whatever changes fall upon the world. Knowledge may widen; thought may deepen; science may alter our outlook upon everything. We may break our way to such stupendous mysteries as our fathers never dreamed of. But always, unshaken and unshakable, stands and will ever stand the Cross of Christ, the one unanswerable proof that God is love.

---

4.   Song of Solomon

"If any man will come after Me, let
him . . . take up his cross daily" (Luke 9:23).

29
Cross Bearing

When the Romans crucified a criminal, not only did they hang
him on a cross, but as a last terrible indignity, they made him carry
the cross upon his back. Probably Jesus, when a lad, had been a
witness of that dreadful spectacle. How it would sink into His boyish mind, the dullest imagination can conjecture. And that was why
when He became a man, He used the imagery of cross-bearing to
describe all that is bitterest in life. The cross is anything difficult to
bear; anything hard, galling, uncongenial; anything that robs the
step of lightness and blots out the sunshine from the sky. And one
of the primary secrets of discipleship is given in our text: If any
man will come after Me, let him take up his cross daily.

The first implication of our text is that cross-bearing is a *univer-*
sal thing. If *any man* will come after Me—then no one is conceived
of as escaping. In the various providence of God there are things we
may escape in life. There are many who have never felt the sting of
poverty; there are some who have never known the hour of pain.
But if God has His providences which distinguish us, He has also
His providences which unite us, and no man or woman ever escapes the cross. There is a cross in every life. There is a crook in
every lot. There is a bitter ingredient in every cup though the cup be

fashioned of the gold of Ophir (1 Kings 10:11). Our Lord knew that every one who came to Him in every country and in every age would have to face the discipline of cross-bearing. The servant is not greater than his Lord.

The next implication of our text is that cross-bearing is *an individual thing*. If any man will come after Me, let him take up *his* cross from which I gather that crosses are peculiar, separate as personality, never quite the same in different lives. When coins are issued from the Mint, they are identical with one another. Handle them, they are alike; there is not a shade of difference between them. But things that issue from the mint of God are the very opposite of that—*their* mark is an infinite diversity. Some crosses are bodily and some are mental. Some spring from unfathomed depths of being. Some are shaped and fashioned by our ancestors, and some by our own sins. Some meet us in the relationships of life, frequently in the relationships of toil, often in the relationship of home. Were crosses, like coins, issued from the Mint, we should ask for nothing more than human sympathy. That would content us, were we all alike. That we would appreciate and understand. But in every cross, no matter how it seem, there is something nobody else can understand, and *there* lies our utter need of God. No one was ever tempted just as you are, though every child of Adam has been tempted. No one ever had just your cross to carry; there is always something which makes it all your own. And that is why, beyond all human kindliness, we need the eternal God to be our refuge and, underneath, the everlasting arms.

The third implication of our text is that cross-bearing must be *a willing thing*. If any man will come after Me, let him *take up* his cross. Probably our Lord, visiting Jerusalem, had seen a criminal led to execution. He had seen the legionary take the cross and lay it on the shoulders of the criminal. And the man had fought and struggled like a beast in his loathing of that last indignity—and yet for all his hate he had to bear it. Our Lord never could forget that. It would haunt His memory to the end—these frenzied and unavailing struggles against an empire that was irresistible. Did He, I wonder, recall that horrid scene when He forbade His follower to struggle so? Let him *take up* his cross. I had a friend, a sweet and saintly man, whose little girl was dying. She was an only child, much loved, and his heart was very bitter and rebellious. Then he turned to his wife and said: "Wife, we must not let God *take* our child. *We must give her.*" So kneeling down beside the bed together, they gave up their baby—and their wills. My dear reader, I do not know your cross. I only know for certain that you have one. And I know, too, that the way you bear it will make all the difference to you. Your cross may harden you; it may embitter you; it may drive you out into a land of salt. Your cross may bring you to the arms of Christ. Rebel against it, you have still to carry it. Rebel against it, and you augment its weight. Rebel against it, and the birds cease singing. All the music of life's harp is jangled. But take it up because the Master bids you, incorporate it in God's plan for you, and it blossoms like the rod of Aaron (Num. 17:8).

The last implication of our text is that cross-bearing is *a daily thing*. If any man will come after Me, let him take up his cross *daily*. There lies the heroism of cross-bearing. It is not a gallant deed of golden mornings. You have to do it cheerfully and bravely every dull morning of the week. Some disciplines are quite occasional. They reach us in selected circumstances. Cross-bearing is continuous. It is the heroism of the dull common hour. Thank God, there is something else which is continuous, and that is the sufficient grace of Him whose strength is made perfect in our weakness, and who will never leave us nor forsake us.

"What shall I then do with Jesus which is
called Christ?" (Matt. 27:22).

30

(*I*)*hich Is Your Answer?*

One possible answer to this question is: *I shall have nothing to
do with Him at all.* I shall ignore Him and pay no heed to Him. If
He confronts me when I go to church, I shall deliberately avoid the
church. If He steals on me when I am quite alone, I shall do my best
never to be alone. If He meets me in certain companies so that I am
very conscious of His presence, I shall be careful to choose my
company elsewhere. I shall bar every window against Him. Against
His coming I shall bolt my doors. I shall give injunctions to my
lodge-keeper that He is never to have access to my avenue. But the
extraordinary thing about the Lord is (and there are thousands who
can testify to this) that to get rid of Him is utterly impossible. He is
inevitable. He is unavoidable. Just because He is love, He laughs at
locksmiths. As on the evening of the resurrection day, when the
doors are shut, comes Jesus. Just when a man thinks that he is safe,
secure from the intrusions of the Lord, He is there within the circuit
of the life, closer than breathing, nearer than hands or feet.

Another common answer to this question is: *Really I can't make
up my mind.* Folk are in perplexity today and therefore halting
between two opinions. Now I want to say, gently but quite firmly,
that is often a dishonest answer. The difficulty is not in making up

the *mind*. The difficulty is in making up the *will*. There are indecisions that are *not* intellectual—they are moral; they are based on character; they strike their roots into some secret sin. The real problem is not making up; the real problem is giving up. We are all tempted to cloak our moral weakness in the garb of intellectual perplexity. But even when the answer *is* entirely honest, there is one thing that should never be forgotten, and that is the great fact of life that not to decide is to decide against. A man is traveling in a railway train. Shall he get out at such and such a station? He halts between two opinions; really he can't make up his mind. Meantime the train has drawn up at the station and is off again thundering through the dark—and the man has decided *against* alighting there just because he could not make up his mind. Few people calmly and deliberately decide against the Lord. But multitudes do it who never thought to do it by the easy way of not deciding. And while I would rush nobody's decision (just as I would not let anyone rush mine), a wise man will accept his universe and never ignore the great facts of life.

Another common answer to this question is: *I shall accept Him by and by.* I have no intention of dying out of Christ; but meantime I want to have my liberty. Life is sweet; it is a thrilling world; I want the color and music for a little. Leave me the gold and glory of the morning, and I shall settle matters in the afternoon. I trust my readers will not be vexed with me if I call that the meanest of all answers; nobody ever likes to be thought mean. Who that had a loved one on a sick-bed would bring that loved one a bunch of withered flowers? And yet many seem to be perfectly content in the thought of offering Christ a withered heart—and He has loved us with a love that is magnificent, and has died for us upon the Cross, and is the finest comrade in the world. It is true that there is always hope; a man may be saved at the eleventh hour. "Betwixt the stirrup and the ground, Mercy I asked, mercy I found."[1] My fear is not that Christ will mock the prayer that is offered at the eleventh hour. It is that when the eleventh hour comes, a man may have quite lost the power to pray. There are things that we can do at one-and-twenty that are almost impossible at sixty. At one-and-twenty one may be a

1. From "Remains. Epitaph for a Man Killed by Falling from His Horse" by William Camden (1551–1623).

footballer; very rare are the footballers of sixty. And to surrender oneself to the Lord Jesus Christ is a far more intense activity than football. Perhaps that is why at sixty it is rare.

Another answer to this greatest of all questions is the frequent one: *I shall compromise.* I shall give Him a certain place within my heart so far as other interests will permit. I have no intention of being out and out; I am not going to carry my heart upon my sleeve. I shall do my duty and lead a decent life and come to church and be present at Communion. But the strange thing is that the meek and lowly Savior, who was content with a manger and a cottage, *is not content with that.* Offer Him *a* place in your life, and the extraordinary thing is that He refuses it. His peace is never won on such conditions; His joy is never a factor in experience. As Henry Drummond[2] put it once, "Gentlemen, keep Christ in His own place, but remember that His place is the first."

There is perhaps only one other answer. It is: *I accept Him now.* Here and now I yield myself to Him for that is my reasonable service. Paul did that going to Damascus (Acts 9:1–9), and it changed the universe for him. Augustine[3] did that in the quiet garden, and it freed him from the tyranny of vice. There are millions everywhere, right across the world, who, giving that instant answer to the question, have found life and liberty and power. My prayer is that these words of mine may lead to such immediate decision. "There is a tide in the affairs of men which, taken at the flood, leads on to fortune."[4] "Seek ye the Lord while He may be found. Call ye upon Him while He is near" (Isa. 55:6). He will never be nearer than just *now.*

---

2. Henry Drummond (1851–1897), Scottish clergyman and writer.
3. Augustine (354–430), bishop of Hippo in North Africa, early church father and philosopher.
4. From *Julius Ceasar* by Shakespeare.

"One thing have I desired of the Lord, that
will I seek after; that I may dwell in the
house of the Lord all the days of my life, to
behold the beauty of the Lord, and to
enquire in His temple" (Ps. 27:4).

31

Beholding and Inquiring

In this verse so full of riches, we have the spiritual ambition of the
Psalmist, and the notable thing is how his single purpose resolves
itself into two parts. Just as the single seeds of many plants separate
themselves out into two seed-leaves, and just as the sunshine, that
most fruitful unity, breaks up, to put it roughly, into light and heat, so
the spiritual ambition of the Psalmist, of which he is speaking in this
verse, reveals itself under two different aspects. One thing he desires
of the Lord, and then that one thing shows itself as two things. He
yearns to behold the beauty of the Lord and to inquire in His holy
temple from which we gather that beholding and inquiring are but
different aspects of one life, vitally interwoven with each other. They
are not contrary nor contradictory like day and night or cold and heat.
They are related elements in every life that is hungering and thirsting
after God. All the experiences of the soul in its inward rest and never-
ending searching may be summed up in beholding and inquiring.

One notes, first of all, how spiritual life runs down its roots into
beholding. "We beheld His glory, full of grace and truth" (John 1:14).

"Behold the Lamb of God" (John 1:29). There are three desires in the heart of every Christian; one is to run his course with honor. The second is to endure, without embittering, the bitterest that life can bring. The third and deepest of the three is this, to be always growing more like the Master in inward character and outward conduct. Now tell me, what is the gospel way toward the achievement of these deep desires? It is not speculation nor philosophy. It is a way within the reach of every man. To run with honor, to endure the worst, to be changed into the likeness of the Lord—all of them are based upon beholding. "Let us run with patience the race that is set before us, *looking* unto Jesus" (Heb. 12:1). "He endured as *seeing* Him who is invisible" (Heb. 11:27). "We all with open face *beholding* as in a glass the glory of the Lord, are changed into the same image" (2 Cor. 3:18). David was not a dreamer. He did not covet a temple-life of idleness. He wanted to run well and to endure and to be transformed into a glowing spirit. *That* was why, beset by sin, he cried with all the passion of his heart, "One thing have I desired—to behold."

The next suggestion of the words is this, that beholding is always followed by inquiring. We see that in every sphere of life and not only in the region of the spirit. Think, for instance, of the stars as they shone down on prehistoric man. For ages in these dim and distant days, man must have been contented with beholding. But just because he was man, made in the image of God, he could not rest in any mere beholding. He began to wonder and wondering, inquired. What were these lamps glowing in the heavens? Who kindled them? Who kept them burning? Did they rain influence on human life? Did they foretell the destinies of mortals? So man, confronted with the stars of heaven, first beheld the beauty of the Lord and then inquired in His holy temple.

Or, again, think of the world of nature that lies around us in its beauty. Touched with the finger of God, man has *beheld* that beauty in a way no beast has ever done. No dumb creature has any sense of beauty. Scenery makes no difference to them. The oxen, knee-deep in the pasturage, never lift their eyes up to the hills. One great difference between man and beast is this, that man, and man alone in this creation, has beheld the beauty of the Lord. The sunlight as it glances on the sea—the flowers that make beautiful the meadow—the haunting mystery of the deep forest—the loch, the lights and shadows of the glen—such things have touched the heart of man and moved him and thrilled him into song in a way no dumb creature ever knew. Just because man is man, one thing is true of him—he beholds the beauty of the Lord. But just because man is man and not a beast, he never can rest content with mere beholding. There is something in him, the breath of his Creator impelling him to ever-deepening wonder until at last in that wonder he *inquires.* "Hath the rain a father, or who hath begotten the drops of dew? Out of whose womb came the ice? and the hoary frost of heaven, who hath gendered it" (Job 38:28–29)? So science is born and all theology and growing insight into the ways of God—because beholding is followed by inquiring.

There is one other relationship to mention, for without any question David knew it. The gladness of the spiritual life is this, that its deepest inquiries are answered by beholding. Let any man be inquiring after God, for instance, eager to know what kind of God He is, longing to be assured that He is Love so that He may be absolutely trusted—well, there are many ways that such a man may take in the hope of answering that deepest of all questions. He may examine the arguments for God, or he may read biography or history; he may turn to the reasonings of philosophy or rely on the pronouncements of the Scripture. But, my dear reader, there is another way—it is what the Bible calls a new and living way: he can *behold* the beauty of our Lord. He can behold His love and carry it up to heaven and say, "That love of Jesus is the love of God." He can behold His care for every separate soul and lift that up to the heart upon the Throne. He can behold His loyalty to His friends and His pardoning mercy for the guiltiest sinner, and then he can say, *"God is just like that."* Do that, and what a difference it makes. God is no longer cold and unconcerned. He is love. He actually cares. He will never do His children any harm. "We beheld His glory, full of grace and truth, the glory of the only-begotten of the Father" (John 1:14). The agonized inquiries of the heart are answered—by beholding.

"And He went down with them, and came
to Nazareth, and was subject unto them"
(Luke 2:51).

32

On Coming Back Again

That visit to Jerusalem was one of the great hours of the life of Jesus. It must have moved Him to the depths. Often in the quiet home at Nazareth His mother had spoken to Him of the Holy City. And the boy, clinging to her knee, had eagerly listened to all she had to tell. *Now* He was there, moving through the streets, feasting His eyes upon the Temple. He had reached the city of His dreams. Clearly it was a time of vision. "Wist ye not that I must be about My Father's business?" (Luke 2:49). In that moving hour there broke on Him the revelation of His unique vocation. And the beautiful thing is that after such an hour, He quietly went back to Nazareth and was subject to Mary and to Joseph. He drew the water from the well again. He did little daily errands for His mother. He weeded the garden, tended the flowers in it, lent a hand to Joseph in the shop. And all this after that great hour which had changed His outlook upon everything and moved Him to the very depths.

That faithful and radiant way of coming back again was very characteristic of the Lord. We see it later at the Transfiguration (Matt. 17:1–9). That was a splendid and a shining hour when heaven drew very near to earth. Such hours find fitter environment on mountain-tops than on the lower levels of the world. There Moses and Elias talked with Him. There was heard the awful voice of God. There His very garments became lustrous. After such an hour of heavenly converse, you and I would have craved to be alone. Voices would have had a jarring sound; company would have been deemed intrusion. And again the beautiful thing about our Lord is that after such a heavenly hour as that He came right down to the epileptic boy. Instead of the voices of Moses and Elias, the clamor and confusion of the crowd. Instead of the tranquillity of heaven, the horrid contortions of the epileptic. It was the way of Jesus, after His hours of vision, to come right back, whole-heartedly and happily, to the task and travail of the day.

Now, that is big with meaning for us all and is capable of endless application. At this season, for instance, one would think of holidays. Many of my readers have had a splendid holiday favored by weather exquisitely fine. A strong light, says Emerson,[1] makes everything beautiful, and multitudes have found the truth of that. And now, from the "large room" of holidays and the healing vision of mountain and of moorland, they are back to the old drudgery again. It is never easy coming back like that, especially in the vivid years of youth. The "trivial round, the common task"[2] are alien and irksome for a little. But if we are trying to follow the great Master, we can show it not only in our going forth, but by the kind of spirit in which we return. *He* went down and was subject to His parents. He left the hills for the epileptic boy. He did it with that unfaltering faith of His which assured Him that His God was everywhere. And in that radiant spirit of return from the vision to the reality, He has left us an example that we should follow His steps.

The same truth holds with equal force of all the great revealing hours of life. There is often not a little heroism in coming back again to lowly tasks. When love has once come caroling down the highway, it is not easy to get back to drudgery. When sorrow has come and "slit the thin-spun life,"[3] how intolerable, often, is that housework! The hand that knocks the nail into the coffin seems to knock the bottom out of everything, and we are left sometimes,

---

1. Ralph Waldo Emerson (1803–1882), American poet and essayist.
2. From *The Christian Year* (1827), "Morning" by John Keble (1792–1866).
3. From "Lycidas" by John Milton (1608–1674), English poet.

paralyzed and powerless, in a world of phantoms we cannot understand. Some men in such hours take to drink. Some who can afford it take to travel. Some lose "the rapture of the forward view"[4] and settle down in the "luxury of woe."[5] But He who came to lead us heavenward and who drank our bitter chalice to the dregs has empowered us for a better way than that. To take up our common task again, to march to our duty over the newly filled grave, to come back to the detail of the day knowing that this, too, is holy ground—*that* is the path marked out for us by Him who went down and was subject to His parents and who left the mount for the epileptic boy.

Nor can we forget how this applies to the great hours of the spiritual life. For that life, too, has its high revealing seasons when, like the apostle, we are caught up to Paradise. After such hours (and one of them is conversion) men often yearn to do great things for heaven. They want to be ministers; they want to leave the workbench and go abroad to evangelize the heathen. If that be the authentic call of God, it will reveal itself as irresistible, but often the appointed path is otherwise. It is not to go forth in glorious adventure; it is to come back with the glow upon the face—to the old home, the dubious friends, the critical comrades, the familiar faces. It is to tell out *there* all that the Lord has done, not necessarily by the utterance of the lip, but by the demonstration of the life. A Christian does not do extraordinary things. He does ordinary things in extraordinary ways. He makes conscience of the humblest task. He does things heartily as to the Lord. And to come back again with that new spirit to the dull duty and narrowing routine is the kind of conduct that gives joy in heaven.

---

4. From "The Thrush in February," by George Meredith (1828–1909), English poet.

5. From "Anacreontic" by Thomas Moore (1779–1852), Irish poet.

"How knoweth this man letters, having never learned?" (John 7:15).

33

Our Lord as a Student

W hat our text implies is this, that our Lord gave the impression of a student. The Jews as they listened to Him recognized the accent of a cultured, educated man. Our Lord stood up in the Temple and began to speak, and whenever the Lord spoke, a crowd would gather. There was something about Him that compelled attention, though nobody could just say what it was. And the one question that sprang to every lip was, "Whence hath this man letters, never having learned?" He had never been at any Rabbinic school, never graduated from any university. He wore the garments of a common man and was evidently a provincial from Galilee. Yet as they listened to Him they recognized the student, the cultivated, educated man.

It is also a very striking thing that the nearer men got to Him, the more they felt it. It was when men were in closest contact with the Lord that they found, to their cost, His scholarly exactitude. There are people who from a little distance give the impression of admirable scholarship, but whenever you get near enough to them, you are pitifully disillusioned. But nobody who came right up to Christ was ever pitifully disillusioned; what happened was that they were *overcome*.

Think for a moment of the Rabbis. They had given their lives to the study of the Scripture. They had scorned delights and lived laborious days poring over the sacred word of Scripture. Yet never one of them encountered Christ but was beaten ignominiously from the field; our Master was the master of them all. "What," He would say to them, "have ye never read?" (Matt. 12:3, 5; Mark 2:25; Luke 6:3, etc.). How the very question must have rankled. Never read! They had been doing nothing else since they entered the Rabbinic university! Yet the proudest scholar of them all invariably was convicted of incompetence by this strange provincial from Galilee.

Nor did our Lord create that deep impression by any elaborate parade of learning. All parade was abhorrent to His soul. Among the Pharisees learning was largely pedantic, with endless citation of authorities. It had passed out of touch with all reality in its meticulous exposition of the law. And over against that pharisaical pedantry, which was the despair of common people, stands the perfect simplicity of Christ. With what perfect and unfaltering ease He used to handle the most abstruse of themes! With what homely and familiar figures He would lighten what was dark! Where others stumbled, groping in the mists, lost in large polysyllabic words, our Lord moved just like a little child. The last thing the Lord ever would suggest to me is that of a man *groping*. There is such perfect mastery about Him, such ease of conscious and consummate power. And whenever you get anything like that, it is more than the crown and blossom of an intellect; it is the crown and blossom of a life. His intellectual processes were beautiful because His life and character were beautiful. He says, "I come to do Thy will, O God" (Luke 22:42; John 4:34 etc.). Our modern psychology stresses *will* as one of the organs and avenues of knowledge, but our Master knew that long ago.

I like to notice, too, that this so perfect student had always the quiet courage to be Himself, and the quiet courage just to be oneself is one of the finest kinds of courage in the world. I have known many a young minister who might have had an admirable ministry; but then he began imitating somebody, and afterward he might as well have stayed at home. That is one great temptation of a student, to see things through other people's eyes; to see the Bible through Dr. Moffatt's[1] eyes or Shakespeare through the eyes

---

1. James Mofatt (1870–1944), Scottish scholar and Bible translator.

of Mr. Bradley.[2] And one of the glorious things about this Student was that He never saw things through other people's eyes; He always had the courage to be Himself. Trained in the home at Nazareth, steeped in the teaching of the Synagogue, with what tremendous pressure the learning of His day must have been brought to bear on Him. And His refusal to be overborne by the tradition of His time is one of the features of the gospel-story. How fresh His expositions were! How He found the truth that everyone had missed! How He swept aside accepted meanings and reached unerringly the beating heart of things. No wonder that men listening to Him found their hearts begin to burn within them as He talked with them by the way.

That leads me, lastly, to suggest that our Lord never was a leisured student. All that He won from Scripture and from nature was won in scanty intervals of toil. It is commonly supposed from certain inferences that Joseph died when Jesus was still young, and from the way in which He is called "the carpenter" one would take it that the shop was His. So one pictures Him growing up to manhood, the sole support of Mary and the children, working "frae morning sun till dine." Not for Him the leisure of the morning, that golden season for the student; not for Him the "endless afternoon," nor the roomy and large hours of evening. And the marvelous thing is that when at length He went out to His public ministry, He was perfect in intellectual equipment. The world had yielded all her treasure to Him. His mind was stored with the teaching of the fields. He was a perfect swordsman with the sword of Scripture at the very outset of His ministry. And all this, garnered in the years when the daily task was arduous and long, and the hours of happy leisure very few. Some of my readers may be just like that. They may have little leisure for the higher things. Engaged in arduous and exacting toil, their time for study may be very limited. Let them be sure the Master understands. His earthly experience was the same. He has not forgotten on His throne in heaven that He was once the Carpenter of Nazareth.

---

2. Francis Herbert Bradley (1846–1924), English philosopher.

"It is the glory of God to conceal a thing"
(Prov. 25:2).

34

On the Divine Ministry of Secrecy

Among the many ministries of God to arrest and stimulate His children, one of the kindliest and commonest is the attractive power of the secret. When a school-girl has a secret she becomes intensely interesting to her fellows. They wheedle her and coax her and even bribe her to reveal her secret. When the Cabinet is rumored to have a secret, how the newspapers grow hot upon the scent, tracking it with the skill of the American Indian! There is something fascinating in a secret. It makes us eager, curious, and alert. It rouses our interest immediately and quickens our dull hearts into attention. And God, who knows our frame, often arrests and stimulates our hearts by a kindly ministry like that. He says, "Children, are you growing dull? Let us play a game of hide-and-seek together." And then, playing, we forget our dullness and find we are having a delightful time. It is the glory of God to conceal a thing, and He, who is a very loving Father, does it in the interests of His own.

Think how interesting *this world* becomes through that attractive power of the secret. The world would be a dull, dead place without it. God does not scatter coal upon the fields; He hides it in the bowels of the earth. He conceals the iron and the diamonds and buries the pearls under the ocean-floor. And then He says, "Children, let us have a game of hide-and-seek," and He does it because He loves us so and longs to have us quickened to activity. It is the secret of the stars that has led to all the triumphs of astronomy. It is the secret of the strata that has urged men to the study of geology. All science, all discovery, all search for the uninhabitable Poles is the response of man to the challenge of the secret. How the secret of an uncharted land played like a magnet on Columbus![1] How the secret of the sources of the Nile haunted and captivated Livingstone![2] The world ceases to be a dull, dead place and grows fascinating and alluring in that divine ministry of secrecy. Every astronomer out watching the lone night, every chemist in his laboratory, every explorer in the heart of Africa, every philosopher brooding on the infinite is the child accepting the summons of the Father to come and play a game of hide-and-seek, and it is in playing *that* we are so happy.

Again one remembers how the secret adds to the attractiveness of *life*. It would be very difficult to live without it. The boys used to tell us in the war how they came to loathe the long, straight road. Walking is always a somewhat dreary business when the road stretches out for miles ahead. What gives it charm so that we walk alert and sometimes quite forget that we are tired is the surprise and unexpectedness of things. Who knows what we are going to see when we have climbed that little hill—what thatched cottages, what ancestral mansions, what brooks meandering amid their marigolds? And it is *that*, that unexpectedness, that secret hidden in the future that upholds us, and keeps the heart young, and gives not a little of the charm to life. When Abraham fared forth (Gen. 12:1), he knew not whither he was going. Had he known everything that lay before him, would he have started with that gallant heart? When Isaac went to Mount Moriah (Gen. 22:1–14), what an awful journey for the little lad had he known *he* was to lie upon the altar!

Doubtless there are some among my readers who have experienced the very bitterest of suffering. They have had dead sorrows or living sorrows—and living sorrows sometimes are the sorer. And I

---

1. Christopher Columbus (1446?–1506), Italian navigator in Spanish service and traditional "discoverer of America."
2. David Livingstone (1813–1873), Scottish missionary and explorer in Africa.

ask them, could they have traveled radiantly and wakened singing on September mornings but for the divine ministry of secrecy? It is the glory of God to conceal a thing, and He does it because His children are so dear to Him. He does not want the heartbreak of tomorrow to blind us to the sunshine of today. He keeps us interested, alert, alive, free to enjoy and grapple with the day through the beautiful method of the secret. Why people should consult the fortune-teller I utterly fail to understand. To wrest the secret from tomorrow is to wrest the radiance from today. Thank God, we do not take our journey on a road that stretches out for miles before us but on one that winds and disappears and then—suddenly—dips into the hollow.

That unfailing attraction of the secret, too, is one of the charming things in *personality*. We are always interesting to each other because we never fully understand each other. There are books which I have read once, and I never want to read these books again. I have mastered them, exhausted them, moved through and passed beyond their little message. But there are other books, like Shakespeare, like the Bible, that I come back to for the hundredth time, and they are alluring and attractive still. They inspire me, yet they escape me. They come right up to me, yet they elude me. I hear them calling me, but when I follow I am lost in the dark magnificence of forests. And it is *that*, that mysterious element, that inscrutable and secret element, which God has lodged in every human breast. You say, "I know him perfectly." My dear reader, *that* you never do. In the most commonplace and ordinary breast there is something beyond the reaching of your hand—something inscrutable, mysterious, secret, too deep for the sounding of any earthly plummet or any analysis of human brain. That is why we all need God, though our lives be rich in human love. That is why sometimes we are all a little lonely, though we be honored with a troop of friends. And that is why to the end, we are always interesting to each other—it is the haunting attraction of the secret. The beautiful thing is that God put it there. It is the glory of God to conceal a thing. He wants us to take an interest in each other and to comprehend things *with all the saints*. The world of nature, the journey we all take, the men and women we meet with as we journey—perhaps we have never thought how much they owe to the divine ministry of secrecy.

"Ye cannot hear My word" (John 8:43).

35

There Are Things We Cannot Hear

I should think that when these words were spoken they must have caused a great deal of perplexity. They seemed a contradiction of the facts. There are speakers whom one cannot hear well. It is a common complaint against the clergy. Especially in the open air there are voices that have little carrying power. But I do not imagine for one moment that this complaint was ever made of Jesus. He could be heard on the outer edges of the crowd. Every word He spoke was audible in the clear still air of Galilee. Even the officers had to bear their testimony that never man spoke like this man. And one can easily picture the perplexity of those who that day were round about Him when our Lord said, "Ye cannot hear My word."

So one comes to feel that for our Lord hearing was not a physical activity. It was rather the reaction of the soul on the syllables which fall upon the ear. Just as two men may look at the same scene yet see in it very different things, so may they listen to the same set of words yet hear the most dissimilar suggestions. It was of such hearing, such spiritual receptivity that our Lord was thinking when He said, "Ye cannot hear My word." For it is not with the ear we hear. It is with the character and spirit. It is by all that we have set our hearts upon, by everything that we have struggled for. Every

119

temptation we have ever met, every sin we have ever fought and
mastered determines the kind of thing that we shall hear as we take
our journey through the world. Live meanly and you hear meanly,
though you be listening to the Lord Himself. Live nobly and you
hear nobly, though all that the ear catches is but commonplace.
There is a great responsibility in speaking if for every word we are
to give account; but our Lord was equally aware of the tremendous
responsibility of hearing.

One finds that selective power of personality in one of the best
known of the gospel narratives. For we read in St. John that when
the Father's voice was heard, "some said it thundered, and others
that an angel spoke to Him" (John 12:29). It was the same voice
that broke on every ear, and yet to one it sounded like the angels
and to another there was nothing in it save the roll of the thunder in
the hills. Had the ear been the one instrument of hearing, that diverse record would have been impossible. But these men were not
hearing with the ear; they were hearing by what they were. All their
past, their habit and their trend, their way of taking the common
things of life leapt to the light unconsciously in the interpretation of
the Voice. That is what is happening constantly. Our verdict on
others is our own verdict. Often our judgment of minister or sermon
is really the judgment of ourselves. We are listening, not with the
bodily ear, but with our loves and hates, our grudges and dislikes.
We are listening with the hidden heart. That is why the Master said
so sternly, "Ye cannot hear My word." There was no physical
impossibility. The impossibility was spiritual. Prejudices, jealou-
sies, antagonisms made the real Christ inaudible to them though His
every syllable fell upon their ear.

Then one remembers how in the Gospel of St. Mark our Lord
says, "Take heed what ye hear" (Mark 4:24). That is a very different thing from saying, "Take heed *how* ye hear" (Luke 8:18). There
is a sense, of course, familiar to everybody in which we cannot help
the things we hear. No one can escape the city's uproar when
walking in the city streets. But our Lord knew that many things we
hear really depend upon our character and would never reach us if
we were only different. There are those to whom we would never
dream of gossiping; they do not hear it because of what they are.
Nobody brings them nasty or lewd tales, and *that*, just because of
their known character. So very often the sort of thing we hear

depends on the sort of character we bear, and therefore for what we hear we are responsible. That is why our Lord says, "Take heed *what* ye hear." The kind of thing we hear is an unconscious revelation of ourselves. And that is why, too, looking across His audience to whom His every syllable was clear, He said, "Ye cannot hear My word." "My sheep hear My voice" (John 10:27)—they hear it because they love the Shepherd. They hear it because through faith and love, they are attuned to the message and the meaning. So does our Lord clearly recognize the tremendous responsibility of hearing. It is those who are of the truth that hear His voice (John 18:37).

"My soul thirsteth for God" (Ps. 42:2).

36

The Thirst for God

The Psalmist, when he wrote this, was a fugitive. He was in hiding somewhere across Jordan. He had been driven out by rebellion from Jerusalem, which is the city of the living God. To you and me, rich in the truth of Christ, that would not make God seem far away. And doubtless the Psalmist also had been taught that the Lord was the God of the whole earth. Yet with an intensity of feeling which we of the New Covenant are strangers to, he associated the Lord with locality. Like Goldsmith's traveler when he went abroad, he "dragged at each remove a lengthening chain."[1] He felt that to be distant from his home was somehow to be distant from his Deity. And so, in a great sense of loneliness, out of a thirsty land wherein no waters were, he cried, "My soul thirsteth for the living God."

But when a poet speaks out of a burning heart, he always speaks more wisely than he knows. When the soul is true to its own prompting, it is true to generations yet unborn. In the exact sciences you say a thing, and it keeps forever the measure of its origin. But when an inspired poet says a thing, it endlessly transcends its origin. For science utters only what it knows, but poetry utters what it feels,

---

1. From *The Vicar of Wakefield*, by Oliver Goldsmith (1730?–1774), English poet, playwrite, essayist, and novelist.

and in the genuine utterance of feeling there is always the element of immortality. No one worries about the atoms of Lucretius,[2] but the music of Lucretius is not dead. No one feeds upon the Schoolmen[3] now, but thousands are feeding upon Dante.[4] And the psalmist may have been utterly astray in his measurements of sun and stars, but, taught of God, he never was astray in the more wonderful universe of soul. That is why we can take his local words and strip them of all reference to locality. True to the deepest in himself, he was true to the deepest in us all. For there is not one of us, whatever be his circumstances, who is not an exile beyond Jordan and thirsting for the living God.

Now it seems to me that this spiritual thirst involves the ultimate certainty of God. It is the one assurance that is never antiquated, the only argument that never fails. I thirst for water, and from a thousand hills I hear the music of the Highland springs. I thirst for happiness, and in the universe I find the sunshine and the love of children. *I thirst for God.* And to me it seems incredible that the universe shall reverse its order now, providing liberally for every lesser craving and not for the sublimest of them all. I do not think that is how things are built. We live in a reasonable order. I do not think, if such had been the universe, that Christ would have said, "Seek, and ye shall find" (Matt. 7:7). For then we should have sought the lesser things and found them to our heart's content; but when we sought the greatest things of all, we would have been hounded empty from the door.

That is why the Psalmist in another place says, "The fool hath said in his heart there is no God" (Ps. 14:1)—there are men who have said that and not been fools. They have said it with aching hearts and ruined homes. They have said it when love had proved itself a treachery. For sometimes the seeming cruelty of things and the swift blows that shatter and make desolate have blotted out even from noble hearts the vision of the Father for a little. God never calls these broken children fools. He knows our frame and remembers we are dust. He is slow to anger and of great compassion, and

---

2. Lucretius (97?–54 B.C.), Roman poet and philosopher.
3. Medieval proponents of scholasticism which included Anselm, Abelard, and Thomas Aquinas.
4. Dante Alighieri (1264–1321), Italian poet.

He will shine upon these shadowed lives again. But the fool has said in his *heart* there is no God. He scorns the verdict of his deepest being. He believes his senses which are always tricking him. He has not the courage to believe his soul. A man may say in his *mind*, "There is no God," and God may forgive him and have mercy on him. But only a fool can say it in his *heart*.

This thirst for God is sometimes very feeble, though I question if it ever wholly dies. You may live with a man for months, perhaps for years, and never light on that craving of his heart. But away in the ranches of the West there are rough men who were cradled in our Scottish glens, and you might live with them for months, perhaps for years, and never learn that they remembered home. Only some evening there will come a strain of music—some folk song, some old northern melody—and on that reckless company there falls a quietness, and they cannot look into each other's eyes just then; and *then* it takes no prophet to discover that the hunger for the homeland is not dead. There are feelings that you can crush but cannot totally destroy, and the thirst for the living God is one of these. You may blunt and deaden the faculty for God, but so long as the lamp burns it is still there. It was that profound and unalterable faith which made our Lord so hopeful for the most hardened sinners of mankind.

And then remember, and with this I close, that *men may thirst for God and never know it.* That eminent scientist Romanes[5] tells us that for five-and-twenty years he never prayed. He was crowned with honor in a way that falls to few—and all the time there was a something lacking. It was not the craving of a noble mind that feels every hour how much is still to do; it was the craving of a noble soul that never knew it was yearning after God. Then, in the embrace of love, they met, and meeting, there was peace. So is it often when souls are very restless. They are craving for they know not what. And all the time, although they little dream of it, *that "know not what" is God.* For as Augustine told us long ago, God has made us for Himself, and we are restless until we find our rest in Him.[6]

---

5. George John Romenes (1848–1894), English biologist.

6. The *Confessions*, Bk. 3, chap. 1.

"No man, having put his hand to the plough, and looking back, is fit for the kingdom of God" (Luke 9:62).

37

On Holding to It

The thought of holding to things doggedly was one of the controlling thoughts of Jesus. That was why He singled out the plowman. Plowmen are not usually learned persons, nor are they often poets in disguise. But there is one virtue they possess pre-eminently, and that is the virtue of quietly holding to it. And it is because in Jesus' eyes that virtue is of supreme importance that He wants us to take the plowman for our model. "If ye *continue* in My word," He says, "then are ye My disciples indeed" (John 8:31). Something more than receiving is required if we are to reach the music and the crown. To hold to it when all the sunshine vanishes and there is nothing but cloud across the sky, *that* is the great secret of discipleship.

We see that with peculiar clarity when we meditate on the great word *abide*. That was one of the favorite words of Jesus. With those deep-seeing eyes of His He has discerned the wonder of the vinebranch. The branch was there abiding in the vine not only in the sunny days of vintage. It was there when shadows fell, and when the dawn was icy, and when the day was colorless and cloudy, and when the storm came sweeping down the glen. Through all weathers, through every change of temperature, through tempest and

through calm, the branch was there. Night did not sever that intimate relationship. Winter did not end that vital union. And our Lord
recognized that as in the world of nature this is the secret and the
source of fruitfulness, so is it also in the world of grace. To abide is
not to trust merely. To abide is to continue trusting. It is to hold to
it—and hold to Him—through summer and winter, through fair and
stormy weather. Nothing could better show the Master's vision of
the great and heavenly grace of holding to it than His love for that
great word *abide*.

Not only did our Lord insist on this; He emphasized it in His life.
For all His meekness, nothing could divert Him from the allotted
path of His vocation. Think, for instance, of that day when He was
summoned to the bed of Jairus' daughter (Mark 5:22–24, 35–43;
Luke 8:41–56). In the crowded street a woman touched Him, and
He instantly felt that "virtue had gone out of Him" (Mark 5:30). But
the original is far more striking in the light it sheds upon the Lord—
He felt that *the power* had gone out of Him. All of us are familiar
with such seasons when power seems to be utterly exhausted. In
such seasons we cannot face the music; the grasshopper becomes a
burden. And the beautiful thing about our Lord is how, after such
an experience as that, He held to it in quiet trust on God. He knew,
in all its strength, the recurring temptation to give over. He had to
reinforce His will continually for the great triumph of continuing.
Through days of weakness, through seasons of exhaustion, through
hours when His soul was sorrowful unto death, He held to the task
given Him of God. It is very easy to hold on when we are loved and
honored and appreciated; when our strength is equal to our problem; when the birds are singing in the trees. But to hold to it when
all the sky is dark is the finest heroism in the world, and *that* was
the heroism of the Lord.

Nor is it hard to see where He learned this, living in perfect
fellowship with heaven. For few things are more wonderful in God
than the divine way He has of holding to it. The ruby "takes a
million years to harden." The brook carves its channels through
millenniums. It takes many months of quiet growth for the ripening
of every harvest. And if we owe so much in the beautiful world of
nature to what I would call the doggedness of heaven, how much
more in the fairer world of grace. We are saved by a love that will
not let us go. Nothing less is equal to our need. We often think that

God has quite forgotten us, and then we discover how He is holding to it. Through all our coldnesses and backslidings, through our fallings into the miry clay, He has never left us nor forsaken us. When we awake we are still with Him, and what is better, He is still with us—just as ready to pardon and restore us as in the initial hour of conversion. No wonder that our Lord in perfect fellowship with such a Father, laid His divine emphasis just there.

For (just as our heavenly Father does) we win our victories by holding to it. We conquer not in any brilliant fashion—we conquer by continuing. We master shorthand when we stick to shorthand. We master Shakespeare when we stick to Shakespeare. Wandering cattle are lean kine[1], whether they pasture in Britain or in Beulah. A certain radiant and quiet doggedness has been one of the marks of all the saints for whom the trumpets have sounded on the other side. In the log-book of Columbus there is one entry more common than all others. It is not "Today the wind was favorable." It is *"Today we sailed on."* And to sail on every common day, through fog and storm and with mutiny on board, is the one way to the country of our dreams. Days come when everything seems doubtful, when the vision of the unseen is very dim. Days come when we begin to wonder if there can be a loving God at all. My dear reader, *hold to it.* Continue trusting. Keep on keeping on. It is thus that Christian character is built. It is thus the "Well done" is heard at last.

---

1. cattle

"He is not here; for He is risen. . . . Come,
see the place where the Lord lay" (Matt.
28:6).

38

The Place Where the Lord Lay *(A Word for Easter)*

One does not associate gladness with the grave. That is not the
experience of men. The sepulcher is the quiet home of sorrow
where the tears fall in gentle loving memory. How often, visiting a
graveyard, does one see somebody lingering by a tomb, taking
away the flowers that are withered, tending it with a sweet and
careful reverence. Such ministrants[1] are seldom singing folk with a
great and shining gladness on their faces. They are the children of
memory and sorrow. Summoned to a grave, we know at once that
we are summoned to a place of sadness. Women clothe themselves
in decent black as perceiving the unseemliness of color. And yet the
strange thing is, in the passage now before us, that when the angel
wanted to make these women glad, he bade them come and investigate a grave. He did not drive them from the garden as Adam and
Eve were driven from the garden. He did not bid them try to forget
their sorrow and go out and face their duty in the world. He quieted
their fears and cheered their hearts and turned their sorrow into

---

1. one who ministers

thrilling joy by bidding them investigate a grave. It is one of the
strangest episodes of history. To exaggerate its uniqueness is impossible. It is the only time in all the centuries when a grave is the
triumphant argument for gladness. We make pilgrimages to see
where poets sang or where patriots lived or captains fought their
battles. But the angel said (and it brought morning with it), "Come,
see the place where the Lord lay."

One marvelous thing was that that place was *empty*, though only
the angel knew why it was empty. It had not been rifled of its
priceless treasure—He is not here, He is risen. The Sadhu Sundar
Singh tells of a friend of his who visited Mohammed's tomb. It was
very splendid and adorned with diamonds, and they said to him,
"Mohammed's bones are here." He went to France and saw Napoleon's tomb, and they said to him, "Napoleon's bones are here."
But when he journeyed to the Holy Land and visited the sepulcher
of Jesus, nobody there said anything like that. *That* was the marvelous thing about the place. It thrilled these women to the depths. The
grave was empty! The Master was not there. In the power of an
endless life He had arisen. That empty grave, flung open for inspec-
tion, lies at the back of all the Easter gladness which had transformed and revivified the world. In the rising of Christ all His
claims are vindicated. In His rising His Father's love is vindicated.
His rising satisfies the human heart which needs more than the
inspiration of a memory. The certainty that we have a living friend
who will be with us always in a living friendship springs from the
investigation of a grave. For once, the grave is not a place of sadness. It is the home of song and not of tears. It is the birthplace of a
triumphant joy that has made music through the darkest hours. "He
is not here; He is risen. He has won the victory over the last great
enemy. Come, see the place where the Lord lay."

But not only was the place empty. We are also told that it was
orderly. *There* were the linen clothes lying and the napkin folded by
itself. Now, some have held (and perhaps they are right in holding)
that this reveals the manner of the rising. The napkin still retained
the perfect circle which it had had when wound around His brow.
As if the Lord, awaking, had not laid aside these graveclothes, but
had passed through them in His spiritual body as afterward He
passed through the closed doors. The older view is different from
that, and to the older view I still incline. It is that our blessed Lord,

awaking, had deliberately put all these things in order. And *that*, if
it be the true conception, is in perfect harmony with all we know of
Jesus in the decisive hours of His life. What a quiet authority He
showed! What a majestic and unruffled calm! Look at Him in the
storm or on the Cross. His are no desperate nor hasty victories. And
now, in His victory over the last great enemy, there is the kingly
touch of a sublime assurance. "He that believeth will not make
haste" (Isa. 28:16). Drowning men struggle for the surface. Men
entombed fight to gain their freedom. But the grave of Jesus bore
not a single trace of any desperate or struggling haste. It was orderly. *There* lay the folded napkin. Leisurely calm had marked the
resurrection. It was the quiet triumphing action of a king. Tell me, if
robbers had stolen the body, would they conceivably have left these
things behind? Or, if they had, would they not have torn them off
and thrown them down in a disordered heap? But they were folded,
and everything was orderly, and there was not a trace of confusion
in the grave. He is not here; *He is risen*.

But not only was it orderly; we must not forget that the place was
also *fragrant*. Spices had been strewn around His body, and the
odor of them filled the tomb. The Lord had left the grave, and it was
empty. He had left it, and it was orderly. But is it not full of
beautiful suggestiveness that He had left it *fragrant*? For now, through
Him who died for us and rose again, there is something of fragrance
in the common grave that none ever had perceived before. There is
the hope of a life that lies beyond in the light and love and liberty of
heaven. There is the hope of meeting again those whom we have
lost, and without whom we never can be perfected. There is the
hope of seeing face to face, at last, in a communion that never shall
be broken, the Friend and Master to whom our debt is infinite.

"When they had found Him on the other side of the sea" (John 6:25).

39

Finding Him on the Other Side

When our Lord had fed the multitude, He constrained His disciples to depart. He wanted a season of solitary prayer. The sun set, and the night grew dark, and He was alone with His Father in the hills; and then we read that in the glimmering dawn He came to His own, walking on the sea. Eager to know more of this great wonder-worker, many had lingered by the scene of miracle. They waited for daybreak and then searched for Him, but nowhere could they find Him. And then, says John, boarding the little craft that happened to ride at anchor in the bay, they crossed the lake, still searching for Him, and found Him on the other side. To a deep mystic like St. John, that simple fact was full of meaning. I think St. John laid his pen down then and thought how often it is true of human life that we find Christ upon the other side.

Think, for instance, of the scribes and Pharisees, the religious leaders of the day. They were all "looking for a king, to slay their foes and lift them high."[1] Their great hope was the Messianic hope.

---

1. From "That Holy Thing" by George MacDonald (1824–1905).

131

They were watching and waiting for Messiah. They were eagerly praying for that Coming One who was to right the wrong and set them free at last. And the singular thing is that when Jesus came, the promised Messiah of the race, they found Him—on the other side. He was over against them, antagonistic to them, pouring on them the vials of His "Woe." He was on the side of the "people of the land" whom the Pharisees and scribes despised (John 9:34). I wonder if John was thinking of all that when he took up his pen and wrote that day—they found Him upon the other side.

Or think again of the disciples when the mothers of Salem brought their babes to Jesus. A mother's heart is a very wonderful thing, and it always wants a blessing for the children. I do not doubt the disciples meant it well when they tried to head these mothers home again. What! had their Master not enough to do that He was to be plagued with crying infants? And I question if they ever would forget, though they lived until their hair was gray, how they found Him that day upon the other side. On the side of the feeble little children; on the side of the tender, loving mothers; on the side of the helpless and the frail; on the side of all who coveted His blessing. I wonder if John was thinking of that day, never to be effaced from memory, when he took up his pen and wrote—they found Him upon the other side.

Or think again, changing the figure a little, of those who are tossing in a sea of doubt. Dwell, for example, on St. Thomas. There are those who doubt because they want to doubt; it affords a certain latitude and license. Sometimes it is easier to doubt than to take up the cross and bear the yoke of Christ. But if ever there was a genuine doubter who would have given worlds to have his doubts removed, it was St. Thomas in the resurrection days. For him doubt was an interior agony; it was the dark night of the soul. It clouded the heavens, blotted out the stars, silenced all the singing of the birds. And the beautiful and encouraging thing is this, that when this poor soul had crossed the sea of doubt, he found Christ upon the other side. He found Him to be far more wonderful than he had ever dreamed in the old days of Galilee. He was no longer "Rabbi"—that is, "Teacher." He was "My Lord and my God" (John 20:28). I wonder if John had a thought to spare for Thomas when, long afterward, he took his pen and wrote they found Him upon the other side.

And is not that, when you come to think of it, the spiritual import of His resurrection? One turns, for instance, to Mary in the garden. In that garden Mary was brokenhearted. She thought her Lord was lost and lost forever. Then she heard a footfall on the grass, and the old familiar voice was saying, "Mary" (John 20:16). And what thrilled Mary and changed her night to morning and brought new hope flooding to her heart was that *she* had found Him upon the other side. We speak much about the Cross, and we never can speak too much about the Cross. The Cross is the spiritual center of the universe. The Cross upholds when everything else fails. But the Cross is of little use to me, whether to my soul or my intelligence, except I find Him on the other side. Only then am I sure that God has conquered. Only then am I sure I have a living Savior. Only then am I sure that Christ is justified (1 Tim. 3:16) in the magnificent adventure of His love. That is the triumphing note of the New Testament, not only that the disciples found Him here, but that they found Him upon the other side.

That, too, sums up our hope of heaven. It is all concluded and embraced in that. The rest and joy and liberty of heaven is just "to be with Christ, which is far better" (Phil. 1:23). What heaven may be like, I do not know. Perhaps it is better that I do not know. Eye has not seen and ear has never heard the things that God has prepared for them that love Him (2 Cor. 2:9). But I cherish the abiding hope in grace, that when I have captained my liner across the sea of time, I shall immediately "see my Pilot face to face."[2] Here He is very hard to find sometimes. Often we suppose He is the gardener. We catch the goings of His insistent feet, but Himself He very often hides (Isa. 45:15). But the great hope of the trusting heart is this, that when death comes and brings unclouded vision—we shall find Him upon the other side.

---

2. From "Crossing the Bar" by Tennyson.

"My beloved . . . standeth behind our wall"
(Song of Sol. 2:9).

40

Behind Our Wall, the Beloved

The thought that greets me in this little bit of poetry is that God stands behind our human life. A wall is not unlike our human life. A wall is built just as a life is built, stone by stone, with quiet and constant toil. No man dreams himself into a character; he has to forge and hammer himself into a character. And then a wall, just like our human life, at once suggests the thought of limitation. We are "hedged about and we cannot get out." Now the great assurance of the believing soul is that the Beloved is standing just behind our wall. He stands at the back of life, and in the deeps of life, and amid all the springs of action and of thought. Nor must we forget how often in the Scripture this great and energizing view is given us of God standing behind our human life. "I heard a voice *behind* me," cries Isaiah, "saying this is the way, walk ye in it" (Isa. 30:21). So St. John on Patmos heard a great voice *behind* him saying, "I am Alpha and Omega, the beginning and the end" (Rev. 1:10–11). And then the Psalmist catches up that thought and puts it in his own poetic way: "Thou hast beset me *behind* and before" (Ps. 139:5).

The difficulty of realizing that largely comes from the littleness of things. Our days are all made up of little things. Great experiences come to us but seldom. But I know a little creek down by the

Clyde,[1] an insignificant and tiny pool. No fish save minnows could ever live in it. The children come to it and lave[2] their feet. And yet that little pool is ruled and regulated by the tides of the majestic ocean; behind it is the controlling of the sea. The fall of an apple is a very little thing. It happens a hundred times each autumn day. Yet to Newton,[3] behind the falling apple was the magnificent law of gravitation. And if the God of nature is the God of grace, and if He "formed the world to be inhabited" (Isa. 45:18), why should it not be so with human life? Life is not built like an Aladdin's palace. It is built of common ordinary bricks—of lowly duties, and minute denials, and infinitesimal and unnoted victories. And the beautiful thing is how clearly we discern, as the days go by and life unfolds itself, that the Beloved stands behind our wall.

Again, when things seem quite the same, it is often what lies behind that makes the difference. That is evident in every sphere. I saw last summer in beautiful Strathspey two pools that looked like sisters. Both were hidden in the purple heather. Both had certain mountain-sedges around them. But the one was only the gathering of the rain, and the other was fed by a spring in the Cairngorms, and when the drought came and the long sunny days, it was what lay *behind* that made the difference. Two people say to you, "I'm glad to see you"—the same words and even the same tones. But the one is only the greeting of formality and the other is the utterance of love. What takes these syllables and differentiates them is not anything that lies within them; it is rather everything that lies behind. I suppose all lives are very much the same. Experience is strangely universal. God makes our lives, just as He makes a day, out of a few simple universal elements. The great distinction of experiences, determining their moral and spiritual meaning, lies in what we have eyes to see behind. When we can take our common task and cross, when we can take our bitter and disappointing cup, when we can take the sorrows that come to every heart and say, "My Beloved stands behind the wall," *that* makes an extraordinary difference.

Often, too, it is what lies behind that determines and controls our spiritual peace. A simple illustration will suffice. A man in comfort-

---

1. A river in Southern Scotland.
2. wash
3. Sir Isaac Newton (1642-1727), English philosopher and mathematician.

able, easy circumstances finds he has only sixpence in his pocket. Leaving home in the morning, he has forgotten his money, and he finds he has only sixpence in his pocket. But that does not trouble him in his familiar neighborhood; he smiles at his folly but is not the least uneasy. He never dreams of forfeiting his peace. But now think of the man who is in beggary. He has only sixpence in the world. He has to get his supper with it and his bed, and then tomorrow morning he will have nothing. The same coin of precisely the same value—it is what lies *behind* that makes the difference, distinguishing between anxiety and peace. The point is, what lies behind our life? Is it chance? Is it fate? Is it the clash of forces? If so, then spiritual peace becomes impossible, and life is under the tyranny of fear. But if God be there in all a father's love, if our Beloved stands behind the wall, *that* makes all the difference in the world.

And that is one of the wonderful things about the Bible. It always sees God behind the life. There is not a single biography in Scripture of which this is not pre-eminently true. Take the story of Joseph or of Abraham. Read the life of Jacob or of David. Through sorrows, sins, journeyings, disappointments, does not the Beloved stand behind the wall? He may encourage, He may guide, He may extricate, He may chastise, but He is always there. What was behind Pilate? Was it the mighty power of the Roman Empire? "Thou couldst have no power at all unless it were given thee by God" (John 19:11). What an upholding and inspiring thought it is, especially for all whose lives may be walled in, that "My beloved standeth behind our wall"!

The Parable of the Prodigal Son
Luke 15:11–32

41

The Two Petitions of the Prodigal

I wonder if my readers ever noticed that the Prodigal made two petitions to his father. The first was: "Father, *give me*." "Give me the portion of goods that falleth to me." The son was growing weary of the home. He felt acutely that he was missing things. The world was big, and the days were going by, and he was young, and he was missing things. It is always bitter, when the heart is young and the world is rich in visions and in voices, to dwell remote and feel that one is missing things. The fatal mistake the Prodigal made was this—he thought that all he wanted was far off. He thought that the appeasing of his restlessness lay somewhere over the hills and far away. He was destined to learn better by and by; meantime he must have every penny for his journey, and he came to his father and said, "Father, *give me*." Mark you, there is no asking of advice. There is no consulting of the father's wishes. There is no effort to learn the father's will in regard to the disposition of the patrimony. It is the selfish cry of thoughtless youth, claiming its own to use just as it will: "Father, give me what is mine."

So he got his portion and departed, and we all know the tragic consequences, not less tragic because the lamps are bright, and the

wine sparkling, and the faces beautiful. The Prodigal tried to feed
his soul on sense; and the Lord, in that grim way of His, changes
the cups, the music, and the laughter into the beastly routing of the
swine. Then the Prodigal came to himself. Memories of home began to waken. He lay in his shed thinking of his father. Prayers
unbidden rose within his heart. And now his petition was not, "Father, *give* me." He had got all he asked, and he was miserable. His
one impassioned cry was, "Father, *make* me." "Father, make me
anything you please. Make me a hired servant if you want to. I have
no will but yours now. I am an ignorant child and you are wise."
Taught by life, disciplined by sorrow, scourged by the biting lash of
his own folly, insistence passed into submission. Once he knew no
will but his own will. He must have it, or he would hate his father.
Once the only proof of love at home was the getting of the thing
that he demanded. But *now*, "Father, I leave it all to thee. Thou art
wise; I have been very foolish. Make me—anything thou pleasest."

And surely it is very noteworthy that it was *then* he got the best.
He never knew the riches in the home until he learned to leave
things to his father. When he offered his first petition, "Father, give
me," the story tells us that he got the money. He got it, and he spent
it; in a year he was in rags and beggary. But when the second
petition, "Father, make me," welled up like a tide out of the deeps,
he got more than he had ever dreamed. "Bring forth the best robe
and put it on him." He got the garment of the honored guest. "Bring
shoes and put them on his feet, and a ring and put it on his finger."
All that was best and choicest in the house, the laid-up riches of his
father's treasuries, were lavished now on the dusty, ragged child.
Insisting on nothing, he got everything. Demanding nothing, he got
the choicest gifts. Willing to be whatever his father wanted, there
was nothing in the house too good for him. The ring, the robe, the
music and the dancing, the vision of what a father's love could be
came when the passionate crying of his heart was, "Father, make
me"—anything You please.

I think that is the way the soul advances when it is following on
to know the Lord. Deepening prayers tell of deepening life. Not for
one moment do I suggest that asking is not a part of prayer. "Ask,
and it shall be given you" (Luke 11:9). "Give us this day our daily
bread" (Matt. 6:11). I only mean that as experience deepens, we
grow less eager about our own will and far more eager to have no

will but His. Disciplined by failure and success, we come to feel how ignorant we are. We have cried "Give," and He has given but sent leanness to our soul (Ps. 106:15). And all the time we were being trained and taught, for God teaches by husks as well as prophets, to offer the deep petition, "Father, make me." He gives, and we bless the Giver. He withholds, and we do not doubt His love. We leave all that to Him who knows us and who sees the end from the beginning. Like the Prodigal, we learn a wiser prayer than the fierce insistence of our youth. It is, "Father, make me"—whatsoever You please.

In closing, might I not suggest that this was peculiarly the prayer of the Savior? The deepest passion of the Savior's heart rings out in the petition, "Father, make me." *Not* "Father give me bread, for I am hungry; give me angels, for I stand in peril." Had He prayed for angels in that hour of peril, He tells us they would have instantly appeared. But, "Father, though there be scorn and shame in it, and agony, and the bitterness of Calvary, Thy will be done; make Me what Thou wilt" (Luke 22:42). How gloriously that prayer was answered, even though the answer was a Cross! God *made* Him (as Dr. Moffatt[1] puts it) our wisdom, that is our righteousness and consecration and redemption. Leave, then, the giving in His hands. He will give that which is good. With the Prodigal and the Savior of the Prodigal, let the soul's cry be, "Father, make me."

---

1. James Moffat (1870–1944), Scottish scholar and Bible translator.

"A certain Samaritan, as he journeyed,
came where he was" (Luke 10:33).

42
Just There

Our Lord, true poet that He was, had a great liking for pictorial teaching, and in all the pictures of His gallery none is more remarkable than this one. The scene, familiar to them all; the robbery, an occurrence they all dreaded; the ecclesiastics, whom they knew so well; the Samaritan, whom they all despised—these made a glowing, vivid picture which nobody but a master could have painted, and nobody but *the* Master ever did. It is a beautiful etching of benevolence, and as such it is immortal. But men have loved, right down the ages, to find in it something more than that. They have loved to find in this Samaritan a delineation of the Lord Himself in His infinite compassion for mankind. Many thoughts come leaping to the mind when we set the story in the light of Christ. This Samaritan was long of coming. He had everything the man required (v. 34). But there is another beautiful feature in his pity that is so eminently true of Christ that we do well to dwell on it a little.

That feature is that the Samaritan came *just where the man was*— came right up to him and handled him where he lay battered on the hedge-bank. When he saw as he came down the hill that in the hollow yonder there had been a struggle—when he saw that battered figure by the road with the robbers probably in concealment, how naturally he might have halted until some Roman convoy had come up; but, says Jesus, he came just where he was. I feel sure our Lord intended that. Christ was unrivaled in suggestive phrase. The Priest *saw* him; the Levite *looked at* him; the Samaritan *came right up where he was.* How perfectly that exquisite touch applies to the Lord, who was the teller of the story, in His infinite compassion for mankind!

Think for a moment of the Incarnation. Tell me, what *was* the Incarnation? It was the Son of God seeing the need of man and coming in infinite mercy where he was. *Not* speaking as by a trumpet from high heaven; *not* casting down a scroll out of eternity; *not* sending Gabriel or any of the angels to proclaim the loving fatherhood of God. No, *this* is the glory of the Incarnation, that when man was bruised and battered by his sin, Christ, the Son of God, the good Samaritan, came just where he was. He came to the inn where the travelers were drinking; to the cottage where the mother prayed; to the village where the children romped; to the fields where happy lovers wandered. He came to the marriage feast and to the funeral, to the crowded city and the sea; He came to the agony and to the Cross. Show me where folk are lying ill at home, and I can show you Jesus there. Show me where men are tempted of the devil, and I can show you Jesus there. Show me where hearts are crying out in darkness, "My God, why hast Thou forsaken me?" and the beautiful and amazing thing is this—that I can show you Jesus there. Where man has suffered, Jesus Christ has suffered. Where man has toiled, Jesus Christ has toiled. Where man has wept, Jesus Christ has wept. Where man has died, Jesus Christ has died. He has borne our griefs and carried our sorrows and made His grave with the wicked in His death. The good Samaritan has come *just where he was.*

And when we follow the footsteps of the Lord, does not the same thing at once arrest us? Why, that is just what the people marked in Christ when they contrasted Him with John the Baptist. If you wanted John, you had to search for John. You had to leave the city and go into the wilderness. And there, "far frae the haunts of men," was John the Baptist, a solitary figure. But Christ was genial, kindly, and accessible, a lover of the haunts of men, the friend of publicans and sinners. Simon Peter was busy with his nets, and Christ came where he was. Matthew was seated at the receipt of custom, and Christ came to him. The poor demoniac was in the graveyard, there to be exiled until he died, and the glorious thing about *our* good Samaritan is that he came exactly where he was.

Where is that bright girl from Jairus' home? We have been missing her happy smile these days. Where is Lazarus? We used to see him daily. Is he ill? We never see him now. Where are the spirits who were disobedient at the time the ark was a-preparing? I know not; I only know of each of them that Christ came *where he was*. Go to the penitent thief upon the cross and tell him there is someone who can save him. Only he must come down and leave the city and fly to the wilderness, and he will find him. There are many who offer Paradise on these terms—when men are powerless and cannot move a finger; but Christ came where he was. That is exactly what He is doing still. Behold, I stand at the door and knock (Rev. 3:20). No one needs to fly away to find Him. The Word is nigh thee, even in thy mouth (Rom. 10:8). "Just as I am," is a very gracious hymn; but I want someone to write me another hymn: "Just *where* I am, O Lamb of God, You come."

"They had the hands of a man under their wings on their four sides" (Ezek. 1:8).

43

The Hands Beneath the Wings

The visions of Ezekiel are often hard to understand, and in part they are hard to understand because of their minuteness of detail. Some men, when they have visions, see things in a hazy kind of way. Ezekiel, when *he* had visions, saw things with remarkable minuteness. And it has always seemed to me that this minuteness, so characteristic of many Bible visions, is a singular attestation of their truth. Many of us recall moments in our life, not infrequently hours of tragic tidings, when we were stunned and seemed to feel nothing save that life would never be the same again. Yet now, as we look back upon these moments when we were far too dazed to comprehend, the marvelous thing is how we recollect the smallest and most trifling detail. So is it with the greatest visionaries. In the intense light everything is photographed. Deep experience resolves itself, through time, into vivid recognition of particulars. And so Ezekiel, thrilled with the glorious vision of these majestic and four-winged cherubim, saw the man's hands under the wings. Do we see anything like that as we look abroad with open eyes? It always seems to me we do.

We see it first *in human life*. Think, for example, of the life of genius, and more especially of literary genius, as exhibited by the great poets. One reads, let me say, some noble poem; it may be the "Divine Comedy" of Dante, or Spenser's "Faërie Queene," or Milton's "Paradise Lost," or the "Endymion" of Keats. Immediately, in the wizardry of art, one is carried away to an ideal world where everything is clothed in perfect beauty. How a true poet soars! How he mounts up with wings as eagles! How he unfurls his pinions to the morning, "above the smoke and stir of this dim spot."[1] And then one reads the story of his life, how he suffered, how he was tempted, how he starved, and there are *the hands of a man under the wings.*

Did you ever read the "Lives of the Poets" by Dr. Samuel Johnson—a book rich in massive wisdom, however inaccurate in particulars? Read it, and you read a story of such captivating and enthralling interest as no novelist ever has conceived. Here are men who had to fight with want, who were the nightly bedfellows of misery; men who seemed to be born to be unhappy, who loved unwisely and were brokenhearted. And then you turn to their poetry again, and how much more wonderful it all appears because of the hand of a man under the wings.

So is it with genius. So is it often with the lives of common folk. Men seem isolated and far away. They wrap themselves around with their wings as did the cherubim. And then bereavement comes to them, or failure, or a season when all the deeps are broken up; and we see what we never saw before. A tenderness we never dreamed of; a touch of nature that makes the whole world kin; a stretching of fingers to grasp us and to clasp us in the great and mystic brotherhood of sorrow. We have our vision then. We understand. We have been judging wrongly all the time. *Now*, like Ezekiel at Chebar, we see the hands of a *man* under the wings.

Not only do we see this in life, we see it also *in all true religion.* All true religion has got wings, but there are the hands of a man beneath the wings. There is a kind of religion that has only wings. It spurns the earth and soars away to heaven. It wings its flight to the everlasting mysteries and is reckless and regardless of humanity. And there is a religion that has only hands. Its passion is the service of humanity. It is summed up in the creed of being kind. But a religion without wings is the most hopeless and ineffectual of reli-

---

1. From "A Mask" by John Milton.

gions. It is like a moorbird I once saw with its wing broken, and the pathos of it I never shall forget. The glory of true religion lies in this, that it mounts heavenward on wings as eagles—but always there is a hand under the wings. First the vision, then the service. First the flight to God, and then humanity. First the poise of the soul amid eternal things—the life that is hid with Christ in God. *Then* the kindly heart, the willing hand, the helping of the lame dog over stiles,[2] the passion for the uplift of humanity.

Some time ago a mother in our mission district was talking to me about her daughter. With a contempt she hardly could conceal she said, *"Mary has no hands."* It was the mother's judgment on her daughter, and one has only to read a certain kind of literature to see that it is the world's judgment on the Church. All true religion *must* have hands—hands to fight and toil for the oppressed; but the hands are ineffectual and powerless unless they be like the hands Ezekiel saw. If human kindness is to bear its fruit, if social service is to be sustained, *first* there must be living faith in God and endurance drawn from seeing the invisible.

Not only do we see this in religion. We see it also *in our Lord.* No cherubim break upon our vision now, but we see Him, and this is true of Him. He was separate from sinners; He confronted men from God's side; He continually beheld His Father's face; He was the Son of Man "who is in heaven." But the beautiful thing, the captivating thing, the thing that has won for Him ten thousand hearts is that beneath the wings were human hands: hands that did not scorn the lowliest service; hands that washed the feet of the disciples; hands that were laid upon the leper; hands that took the piece of bread and brake it; hands that caressed the little children, and gripped Peter when he began to sink, and at last were nailed upon the tree. In the shelter of His wings we trust. He "covereth us with His feathers" (Ps. 91:4). But, exalted to the right hand of power, can we be certain that He understands? Yes, we can always be quite sure of that, for still, beyond the veil and on the throne, there are the hands of a *man* beneath the wings.

---

2. steps

"O woman, great is thy faith" (Matt. 15:28).

44

Great Faith

The greatness of faith often can be measured by the obstacles it overcomes. Our Lord evidently had that in mind when He spoke of the faith of a grain of mustard seed. The mustard seed, when it is grown, is nothing extraordinarily beautiful or useful. One does not love it as one loves the lilies, nor is it fashioned into food for man. The wonderful thing about the mustard seed is its gallant adventure in the world of life, starting from the unlikeliest beginnings. Faith can often be measured by achievement; but achievement is not the only measurement. It may accomplish little and yet be really great in its overcoming of opposing circumstances. And in the faith of this Syrophoenician woman *that* feature is so signal and so splendid that we might measure her faith by that alone. Let us, then, lay aside all else and think only of the things that were against her when she came to Jesus that memorable day.

In the first place, *her birth was against her.* St. Matthew tells us that she was a woman of Canaan, and she is called by St. Mark a Syrophoenician woman from which we learn that she belonged by birth to one of the native races of the land. Now when, long centuries before, the Jews had entered Canaan, they had been bidden to exterminate these races. It had been war to the death between the

Hebrews and the tribes who were in possession of the land. And we know what hatred and what bitterness will rankle in the heart of some poor remnant whose memories are of exterminating wars. Into that heritage was this woman born. She was bred in abhorrence of the name of Jew. To her the Jew was like the Norman conqueror[1] to the disinherited and defeated Saxon[2]. Yet all the bitterness in which she had been trained and the prejudice in which she had been steeped was overcome in her profound belief that Jesus could save her little daughter. How her neighbors would deride her if she hinted to them the nature of her errand! They would charge her with being false to her own gods, a traitress to her people and her past. But all the mocking of her village friends was powerless to dissuade her from her purpose, and here we find her at the feet of Christ.

Again, *her lack of knowledge was against her.* This woman was not a Jew: she was a Grecian. She had been reared in the worship of the heathen gods and was a stranger to the God of Israel. Doubtless she had heard the Lord's name, but always in tones of hatred or contempt. Possibly there had drifted to her ear tidings of the Jewish hope of a Messiah. But how that hope would be misrepresented and in what distorted fashion it would reach her is not very difficult to picture. She was a stranger to the Hebrew Bible with its prediction of a coming Savior. She had never dwelt upon its page in secret, feeding her soul on the nurture of the promises. The Psalms of David she had never sung; the fifty-third of Isaiah she had never read; no one had ever told her of a Coming One who was to bear the sicknesses of others. Think, too, how little she could know of Christ Himself. It is almost certain that she had never seen Him. A woman with such a heart and such a daughter was unlikely to be much from home. All that she knew of Jesus was from hearsay from the stray rumors that would travel northward, and there was not a single rumor yet that could speak to her of the healing of a heathen. When the sisters sent for Jesus when Lazarus was ill, theirs was indeed a noble faith. But Christ had lived with them and loved them, and all that was a mighty encouragement to faith. Here there was nothing of such sweet experience; no personal knowledge for faith to strike its roots in. And it was all so wonderful that even Jesus wondered—"O woman, great is thy faith."

Once more, *the disciples were against her*—"Send her away, for

---

1. Conquest of England under William the Conqueror in A.D. 1066
2. Sixth-century Germanic settlers in Britain.

she crieth after us." They had come northward for a little rest, and they were irritated at being so disturbed. Perhaps what they meant was this: "Give her the boon she craves, and let her go. The crowd will be sure to gather at her cries—for the sake of peace grant her request." But the very fact that they could speak so shows that they viewed her in an unkindly light and, from the moment that they saw her, had cast upon her uninviting looks. So had they acted with the mothers of Salem when *they* brought their little ones to Jesus (Mark 10:14). How much more natural such conduct now, when the mother was a Syrophoenician and a heathen. Yet all the angry looks of the disciples, and their biddings that she should hold her peace, and their drawing together to keep her off from Jesus, and the fact that they were men and she a woman—all this was powerless to dishearten her or to quench the shining of her faith.

But there was one other obstacle she had to conquer, *for Christ Himself seemed to be against her.* When she pleaded with Him in all her mother's passion, He answered her never a word. These silent lips were terrible enough—they were so unlike all she had heard of Him; but when He spoke it was like the knell of doom robbing her of the hope that was her life: "I am not sent but unto the lost sheep of the house of Israel" (v. 24). Do not imagine it was said to try her. It was said in the perfect sincerity of truth. There is an order in the plans of God, and the time of the Gentiles was not yet. But what did the woman do—did she retire? Did she say, "Ah me, my case is hopeless now"? There is something magnificent in what she did—she came and worshiped and cried to Him, "Lord, help me" (v. 25).

Again Jesus raised another obstacle. He uttered that dark word about the dogs—not the wild and masterless dogs of Eastern streets, but the "doggies" which even then were household pets. And the alertness, the ready mother-wit with which this mother parried that rebuff is one of the most delightful things in Scripture. Who could have blamed her if, being called a dog, she had turned in womanly anger and gone home? Instead of that she catches up the words and turns the supposed taunt into an argument. And it was then that Jesus, charmed and captivated by that refusal to admit defeat, crowned her with the commendation of our text. Her birth was against her; her knowledge was against her; the Twelve were against her; Christ *seemed* to be against her. But her great faith broke every obstacle—and her daughter was made whole that very hour.

"I will love him, and will manifest Myself
to him. . . . We will come unto him and
make our abode with him" (John 14:21, 23).

45

The Ladder of Promise

Out of all the riches of these verses let us take what the Lord says
about Himself. Let us select the words He uses of Himself. We may
not disentangle in experience the acting of the Father and the Son, but
often we may disengage in thought what we cannot disentangle in
experience. So here we may reverently lay aside, in thought, what the
Lord says about the Father and think only of what He says about
Himself. When we do that, how beautiful it grows! We see a gradually ascending scale of promise. We see the Master adding thought to
thought until He reaches at last a magnificence of climax. And all this
in glorious response to the great waves of doubt and of depression
which must have rolled over the hearts of His disciples. Let us try,
then, to view this ladder of promise from *their* standpoint.

I take it that the primary dread within their hearts was that,
departing, He would cease to love them. He was going away far
beyond their ken, and His love would be nothing but a memory. So
long as He had companied with them, His love had made all the
difference in the world. It had wrapped them around and sheltered
them. It had been their refuge and their tower. Now He was about to
leave them—to pass over into another realm—and that love would

be nothing but a memory. They knew perfectly that for full rich life something more than memory is needed. Left with memories of love and nothing more, how could they be strong to face the future? And then the Lord said (for He knows our thoughts), Children, *I will love you*, in the future just as in the past. His love was not to cease when He was slain. It was not to cease when He went home to heaven. It was to be as real, as watchful, and as comforting as in the dear dead days beyond recall. What a joyful message for these poor disciples, aware that something awful was impending, dreading the bitter thought of separation!

Then would follow another wave of doubt: He will love us, but shall we ever know it? Separated from us and far away in glory, if He loves us, shall we be conscious of it? Many a congregation loves its minister, but it never tells him of that love. Many a Scottish husband loves his wife, but the years go by and the husband never utters it. And I suppose the disciples, in that parting season when their Lord assured them He would love them still, fell to doubting if they would ever know it. When He was with them, they knew it every hour. He showed His love in innumerable ways. *Now* He was going home, and though He loved them still, would there be any apprehension of that love? And it was then that the Lord, the Master of the heart and of all the swift questionings of the heart, said, Children, *I will manifest Myself to you*. That is, not only was He going to love them, but He was going to show them that He loved them. He was going to make His love as clear and manifest as in the days when He walked with them in Galilee. And one can picture the gladness of His own and the new light that would leap into their eyes when they heard that second promise of their Lord.

But a new wave was on the point of breaking. Doubts and difficulties had not vanished yet. Would the showing of His love include His presence?—if not, the past was richer than the future. Men can tell their love by letter. They can tell it and be a thousand miles away. Many a young fellow in the war did that, and the letters are cherished to this hour. At home and moving through the house, they never told their mothers how they loved them; but they wrote it from France or from Gallipoli[1]. Now try to get inside the hearts of the disciples; theirs were hearts extraordinarily like our own. Would

---

1. Gallipoli, Turkey, site of major Allied defeat in World War I, April 1915.

not they instantly begin to speculate how the Lord was going to show His love? And I daresay, being Jews, they thought of the mediators of the ancient law and began dreaming of angelic messengers. Tidings would be flashed from far away. White-robed ministers would bring the news. The Lord, remote in the land of the far distances, would have His means of showing that He loved them. And immediately every one of them would feel that this was something less than the dear past when they had His presence in the fields of Galilee. Then, in early morning, He had come to them. He had come to them across the sea. He had come in the hour of their utmost need as from the mountain of Transfiguration. And our blessed Lord, understanding perfectly these thoughts that were surging in their hearts, said thirdly, Children, *I will come to you.* I am not going just to send a message telling you that My love is still unaltered. I am not going to commission any angel. As in the old days, now drawing to a close, when My presence went with you and gave you rest, I am going to come to you *Myself.*

But when we love anybody very much, it is not enough that he should come to us. We want him—do we not?—to stay with us. Now, then, think of these disciples. The Lord had promised that He would come to them. But if He came and swiftly went away again, how their house would be left unto them desolate! And yet what more could *they* expect, a little band of very lowly folk, now that their Master was the King of glory? If the government was on His shoulder, if He was seated at the right hand of power, if He was in control of the whole universe and Captain of the hosts of heaven, how much of His time could *they* expect, a little handful of humble Galileans? At the most, a brief glance, a passing word—and before, they had had Him all the time. At the most, a coming for a few blessed moments, followed by the sadness of farewell.

And then the Lord, reading all their thoughts and, it may be, smiling at their childishness, said, Children, *I will abide with you.* I will love you. Yes, Lord, we believe it, but what if we should never know it? I will show My love to you. Yes, Lord, we believe it, but You might be very far away and show it. I will come to you. Yes, Lord, we believe it, but think of the darkness when You go away again. Foolish children, *I will abide with you.* There is nothing more to be said. It is all there. Love's questionings and anxieties are silenced. The ladder of promise is complete.

"The generation of Jesus Christ"
(Matt. 1:1).

46

The Setting of the Pearl

It is generally agreed that the Gospel of St. Mark is the earliest of
the four Gospels, and it is notable that in this earliest Gospel there is
no genealogy at all. St. Mark does not give the ancestry of Christ
nor does he say a word about His lineage. He stands beside the
flowing river and never seeks to trace it to its source. St. Mark,
from the very outset, has his gaze fixed upon the Savior and brings
the reader face to face with Him. There is no attempt to explain the
fact of Christ by relating it to the long past. All that will come in
season, for unrelated facts can never satisfy. The *first* thing is to
have Jesus shown us, to be confronted with Him as a living person,
and that is the divine office of St. Mark.

But just because man is a reasonable being, he can never find
rest in isolated facts. And in the next Gospel, the Gospel of St.
Matthew, you have our Lord related to the past. St. Mark plunges
into the heart of things. He confronts you with the Savior. He says:
"If you want to understand the Lord, the first thing is to fix your
gaze on Him." Then St. Matthew takes that isolated fact and traces
it back to David and to Abraham; Christ is "the son of David, the
son of Abraham" (1:1). St. Matthew is thinking out what Christ
implies, the Christ who had changed His life down to the deeps, and

the great truth which dawns on him is this, that it takes David and Abraham to comprehend Him. In other words, St. Matthew says that if you want to understand the Lord, you must take in the whole of Jewish history. To St. Matthew Christ is the crown of Jewish history. Without Him it is inexplicable. It was to Him that the sacrifices pointed. It was of Him that all the prophets wrote. That is why, for all its difficulties, we never can dispense with the Old Testament. Christ is the son of David, who is the son of Abraham.

Then you come to the Gospel of St. Luke, and in St. Luke you have a larger setting. St. Luke does not trace the lineage to Abraham. He traces it right back to Adam: "which was the son of Seth, which was the son of Adam" (3:38). Beyond the parent of the Jewish race stands the parent of the human race. Beyond the representative of Israel stands the representative of man. And St. Luke sees that to comprehend the Lord calls for more than the history of Israel; it calls for the long story of humanity. Much in Christ will always be unintelligible unless you know the page of the Old Testament. But it takes more than the page of the Old Testament to reach His full significance. Christ is the son of Adam, says St. Luke. He is vitally related to humanity. He is in living touch with all mankind. St. Matthew says: "If you want to understand Him, you must lay your hand upon the Jewish heart." St. Luke says: "If you want to understand Him, you must lay your hand upon the human heart." And one of the beautiful features of St. Luke's Gospel is the stress it lays upon that larger setting—on Christ as the Savior of mankind. The Gospel is full of tender human touches, such touches as make the whole world kin. Roman officers march across its avenues. The Good Samaritan is there. In the Christ of St. Luke there is neither Jew nor Greek, barbarian, Scythian, bond nor free. He is the son of Adam.

Lastly we come to the Gospel of St. John, the last of the four Gospels, written after years of ceaseless brooding on everything the Lord had meant. How then does St. John begin? What is the lineage he gives? Is he content to trace Christ back to Abraham, or to set Him in relationship to Adam? "In the beginning was the Word, and the Word was with God, and the Word was God, and the Word became flesh and dwelt among us" (1:1, 14). St. Mark gives the fact of Christ and bids us start by contemplating that. St. Matthew relates that fact to Jewish history; St. Luke to the whole history of man. Then comes St. John, after the lapse of years, and says, "All that is not enough. If you want to understand the Lord, you must relate Him immediately to God." *That* is the final setting. That the ultimate relationship. The glory of the Man St. John had known is that of the only-begotten of the Father. He comes from Abraham. He comes from Adam. Yes, says St. John, but there is another lineage: the Word was with God, and the Word was God, and *the Word was made flesh, and dwelt among us.*

"Having your conversation honest among the Gentiles" (1 Peter 2:12).

47

On Doing Things Bonnily

T hat word *conversation*, as we all know, has a different meaning on our lips from that which it bears in Holy Scripture. Words are like men and have their history, and sometimes the history leads upward, and sometimes it moves down to meaner things. Conversation on *our* lips just means talk; in the Bible it means the life behind the talk—the general course and tenor of the life, the way that a man has of doing things. Then the word *honest*, while including honesty, has suggestions that honesty does not convey. It is not the Greek equivalent for honest; it is the Greek word for *beautiful*. And so an old Scottish saint and scholar, who was always discovering charming things in Scripture, used to say that what this text means is, *Do things bonnily.*[1] That is to say, it is not enough to *do* things if you are seeking to commend the Lord. You may do the right things in the wrong way. You may do them in a way that causes pain. The mark of the follower of the Lord Jesus is that whatever he has to do in life, like his Lord, he tries to do it *bonnily.*

That our Lord expected this of His disciples is seen clearly in the gospel story. For instance, think of what He said of fasting (Matt.

---

1. well

155

6:16). When hypocrites fast, said the Lord, they do it in an ugly way. Not only do they obtrude their sadness, they make a practice of disfiguring their faces. And the word for disfigure in the Greek is a very interesting word; it means to dim the luster so that the beauty vanishes away. A fasting hypocrite was not a bonny sight, and he did not want to be a bonny sight. He wanted men to know that he was fasting, and he conveyed the information by his ugliness, just as hypocrites to this hour try to show they are "fasting from the world" by deliberate rejection of the beautiful.

Now Jesus, for all His geniality, knew the moral necessity for fasting. He knew that, for natures such as ours, occasional fasting is imperative. His aim was not to discourage fasting; He took it for granted that His own would fast; His aim, here and everywhere, was to discourage ugly ways of doing it. When you fast, He says, anoint your head, give yourself the oil of joy for mourning. Wash off the disfigurement of sadness so that nobody would dream that you were fasting. In other words, what the Lord says is this, "Child; with the seven devils in you, fast; but see to it that you always do it bonnily." The same thing applies to prayer. The same thing applies to almsgiving. How much almsgiving is robbed of grace because of the ugly fashion of its exercise? No right thing is perfect in the Lord's eyes, however unassailable its rightness, unless it is also beautifully done.

This is what profoundly impressed men in the life and walk of our Lord Himself. "We beheld His glory," says the great apostle, "*full of grace and truth*" (John 1:14). Now, grace, whatever else it is, is charm. It may be more; it never can be less. Grace is something exquisitely beautiful, whether on the lips or in the life. And what moved men who had companied with Jesus and what filled them with adoring wonder was that always and in every circumstance they had found Him full of grace and truth. There is a kind of truth that is not charming. It is harsh, uninviting, and repellent. It may be the very opposite of falsehood and yet the very antithesis of love. But the truth in Jesus was a charming thing; it had all the attractiveness of beauty; and men, remembering it, said, "We beheld His glory, full of grace and truth." All the truth He uttered, He uttered beautifully. Men wondered at the words of grace upon His lips. All the truth He did, He did beautifully. He *was* the truth—yet "altogether lovely." And so Peter, writing to these early Christians, says, "Friends, do you want to exhibit Christ among the pagans? Then whatever you do, be sure you *do it bonnily.*"

One might illustrate that from every stage of Christ's life. Just think for a moment of the foot-washing. It is John who tells us of the foot-washing (John 13); it is Luke who interprets its significance. Luke tells us that on the way up to the capital the disciples had been quarreling about precedence. They had been arguing their respective claims to greatness and doing it with heat. Could you have wondered if their Master, angry, had scorched and shriveled them with *truth*? But you see He was full of *grace* and truth. He took a towel. He girded Himself. He poured the water into the basin. Probably without one word, He stooped down and began to wash their feet. And when there flashed on them the truth about themselves, and with it the truth about their Lord, did they not feel He was altogether lovely? He might have healed the leper with a word—instead of that He touched him. When He brought Jairus' daughter back from death, He commanded that something be given her to eat (Mark 5:43). What a beautiful touch; and Peter saw it and seeing it never could forget it; and so he writes, "Do you want to show forth Christ among the pagans? See to it, then, that you always *do things bonnily.*"

That, then, we must always set before us if we really want to commend our blessed Savior. The right things are not wholly right in *His* eyes—unless they are also beautifully done. It is a great thing to give alms. It is a great thing to take up one's cross daily. It is a great thing to be a faithful wife or husband. It is a great thing to help a friend. But "what do ye more than others?" Well, there is one thing more that you can do. For the Lord's sake you can always *do things bonnily.*

"Thy faithfulness reacheth unto the clouds" (Ps. 36:5).

48

The Reach of His Faithfulness

The faithfulness of God is one of the strong truths of the Old Testament. It is one distinction of the Jewish faith in contrast with the ancient pagan faiths. Pagan gods were not generally faithful, whether in Babylon or Greece. They were immoral, careless of their promises, regardless of their plighted word. And the wonderful thing about the Jewish faith was that the God of the Jew was always faithful, both to His covenant and to His children. This magnificent and upholding thought sprang not alone from personal experience. It was interwoven with the fact that the Jewish faith was an historical religion. The Jew could look backward over the tracts of time and discover *there* the faithfulness of God in a way that one brief life might never show. As he recalled the story of the past, of Abraham traveling to the promised land, of the slaves in Egypt rescued from their slavery, of the desert pilgrimage of forty years, one thing stamped upon his heart, never to be erased by any finger, was that the Lord was a faithful God. That thought sustained the psalmist and with him all the saints of the Old Covenant. In the Old Testament the word faith is rare; but the word faithfulness occurs a score of times. And here the psalmist in his poetic way, and like Jesus drawing his images from nature, says, Your faithfulness reaches *to the clouds*.

One thinks, for instance, of the clouds *of Scripture* in such a passage as the Ascension story. When our Lord ascended to the Father, a cloud received Him from the disciples' sight (Acts 1:9). That was a lonesome and desolating hour when the cloud wrapped Him around, and He was gone. They had loved Him so and leaned upon Him so, that I take it they were well-nigh brokenhearted. Then the days went on, and they discovered that the engulfing cloud was not the end of everything. It, too, was touched by the faithfulness of heaven. He had promised to be with them always, and He was faithful to that promise still. He had said: "I will manifest Myself to you" (John 14:21), and that plighted word was verified. The cloud had come and wrapped their Lord around, and they thought the sweet companionship was over. But His faithfulness reached unto the clouds.

Again one thinks of the clouds *of history*, for history has its dark and cloudy days. For instance, what a cloudy day was that when the Jews were carried off to Babylon. Exiled to a distant, heathen land, they thought that God had forgotten to be gracious. They said: "My way is hidden from the Lord, and my judgment is passed over from my God" (Isa. 40:27). It was not the hardship of exile that confounded them. It was that God seemed to have broken covenant and had been found unfaithful to His promises. By the waters of Babylon they sat and wept (Ps. 137:2). They hanged their harps upon the willow-trees. How could they sing the faithfulness of God when He had let them go into captivity? And yet the day was coming when the instructed heart would rise to another view of that captivity, and say: "Thy faithfulness reacheth to the clouds." Memory became illuminative. Things lost grew doubly precious. Distance helped them to a clearer vision of what sin was and what God was. And then across that dark and cloudy day came the ringing of prophetic voices with the message of ransom and return (Isa. 35). They were not forgotten. They were not rejected. Their way was not passed over by their God. Sunny days did not exhaust His faithfulness. It reached even to the clouds. And of how many a dark day of history (as when we revert in thought to the Great War) can we set to our seal that this is true!

Again, one thinks how this great truth applies to the clouds that hang *over our human lives*. What multitudes can say in an adoring gratitude, Thy faithfulness hath reached unto the clouds? Just as in every life are days of sunshine when the sky is blue and all the birds are singing, when every wind blows from where the Lord is, and when we feel it good to be alive; so in every life are shadowed days when the sun withdraws its shining for a season, and the clouds return after the rain.

It may be the time of trouble in the family or of great anxiety in business, the time when health is showing signs of failing, or when the chair is empty and the grave is full. It may be the time when all that a man has lived for seems washed away like a castle in the sand. It may be the day of unexpected poverty. How unlooked for often are these clouds of life. They gather swiftly like some tropic thunderstorm. We confidently expect a cloudless day, and before eventide the sky is darkened. And yet what multitudes of folk, as they look backward with large experience of life, can take our text and in quiet adoring gratitude claim it as the truth of their experience. *You* thought (do you not remember thinking?) that God had quite forgotten to be gracious. Probably you were tempted to deny Him or secretly to doubt His care for you. But now, looking back upon it all, you have another vision and another certainty, just as the experienced psalmist had. If there be any of those who read these lines for whom *this* is the dark and cloudy day, who are very anxious and distressed, who say in the morning, "Would God that it were evening"—have faith. Do not despond. The hour is nearer than you think when you also will say with David, "Thy faithfulness reacheth *to the clouds*."

"After that He appeared in another form
unto two of them, as they walked, and
went into the country" (Mark 16:12).

49

In Another Form

This is all that St. Mark has got to tell us of our Lord's appearance on the Emmaus road. It is in the Gospel of St. Luke that we have the exquisite story in detail. St. Luke tells us that when He joined the wayfarers, their eyes were holden and they did not know Him. Although when He spoke to them their hearts began to burn, something interfered with recognition. And St. Mark tells us what that something was which kept them from recognizing Jesus—He appeared unto them *in another form*. What that form was we do not know. This is one of the silences of Scripture. The Bible can be magnificently eloquent, and the Bible can be magnificently silent. It was *another*; it was different; it was not any form they were familiar with; and then (as in the play) the rest is silence.

I should like to say that if Jesus be of God, this is exactly what I should expect. The work of God differs from that of man in the beautiful varying of form. Man builds a bridge, and it remains a bridge: it is still a bridge when fifty years have gone. Man constructs the engine for the liner, and that engine never varies until it is scrapped. And then God comes and begins building, and one great mark of His handiwork is this, that it is always appearing in another form. He makes the oak—it is barren in November. It appears in another form in July. He makes the seed, intricate in mystery. It appears in another form upon the harvest-field. He makes the hawthorn, flowering in May and burning with scarlet berries in the autumn. It is the same bush, but in another form. That is particularly true of sunshine, and our Savior is the sun of righteousness. One of the mysteries of sunlight is how it is always appearing in another form—in health, in countless energies, in the coal-fire burning in the grate, in the colors of the lilies of the field. Now, according to my gospel, He who gave the sunshine gave the Lord. God so loved the world that He *gave* His only begotten Son. And I should expect, if Jesus be of God as the sunshine and all the lilies are, that He would appear in another form.

One thinks, for instance, how very true that is of Christ *in succeeding generations*—He is the same, yet the form is ever changing. Suppose that some preacher of a hundred years ago were to "revisit the glimpses of the moon"—an able man, born of the Holy Spirit, consecrated to his heavenly calling. Suppose he were to preach one of his sermons to an audience of our more thoughtful young people; does not everyone know what they would say? They would say, "That is an able man, and we recognize him as perfectly sincere. We admire his logic and we enjoy his eloquence, and we wish we had more of it today. But the Christ he preaches—dogmatic, theological—seems to be out of contact with our lives, and his message (to put it frankly) leaves us cold." Then folk talk of this degenerate age—as if Christ were a man-constructed thing; as if He were like that engine of the liner that can never vary until it is scrapped. While all the time the glorious thing is this, that to every succeeding generation Christ is appearing in another form. Always the same—always the Son of Man—always (as I believe) the Son of God—able to save as no one else can do, for He is able to save unto the uttermost—yet, like the lily and the hawthorn and the sunshine (these glorious but lesser gifts of heaven), too wonderful to be tied to one epiphany.

One thinks again how very true that is of Christ *in different individuals*. That is where He differs from the creed or catechism, however indispensable they be. Your creed or catechism never varies, whether a man be a blackguard or a saint. It meets you with the same form of words when the bells are ringing and when the heart is breaking. But Christ, living, infinitely sensitive to the secret lodged in every separate heart, is always appearing in another form. How different the Christ of the converted criminal from the Christ of the philosophic thinker! How different the Christ of one of Cromwell's Ironsides[1] from the Christ of the delicate and shrinking woman! Right down the ages in our varying lives, you have the transcript of resurrection morning when Mary supposed He was the gardener, and the two saw Him in another form. He came to Paul as the righteousness he craved for. He came to Justin Martyr[2] as the truth. He came to St. Francis[3] as the radiant Comrade. He came to Spurgeon[4] as rest and satisfaction. Always the same, always the Son of Man—always (as I believe) the Son of God, yet in differing form to different personalities, and every form most exquisitely chosen.

One thinks, lastly, how very true this is of Christ *in the advancing years of life*. He is the "very same Jesus" to the end, yet different in form with every mile. *That* is where He is so like the Bible, for this is one of the wonders of the Bible. The Bible we cherish when we are growing old is identical with the Bible of our childhood—yet how different—how rich in new significance—how melodious with notes of heavenly music that we never had ears to hear when we were young. With every trial met and temptation mastered, the Bible appears in another form—with every illness, and every hour of heartbreak, and every cross that we are called to carry. And the wonder of the written word is just the wonder of the Word Incarnate: He is always appearing in another form. In ardent youth, the Lord of high endeavor; in the years of stress and strain, the Lord of rest; in the evening when the first stars come out, the Way that leads us home. And when we waken in the brighter morning, *there* He will be just the same—and yet we shall see Him in another form.

---

1. Soldiers serving under Oliver Cromwell.
2. Justin Martyr (c. 100–165), philosopher and Christian apologist.
3. St. Francis of Assisi (1182–1226), founder of the Franciscan Order.
4. Charles H. Spurgeon (1834–1892), influential English Baptist preacher.

"And about the eleventh hour He went
out, and found others standing idle"
(Matt. 20:6).

50

The Eleventh-hour Man

By the eleventh-hour man I mean the man who at five o'clock is
still outside the Kingdom, and one would notice first that in the
parable there is no hint of this man being *bad*. There was another
eleventh-hour man who had taken to evil courses on the highway.
He had left home and broken his mother's heart, and we see him at
last hanging on a cross. But this man was a much more usual type,
haunting the marketplace in search of work, not forgetful of his
wife and children. If you want the prodigal, go to the far country. If
you want the bandit, take the road to Jericho. Our Lord, in that most
masterly way of His, has always a fitting background for His characters. And this man, against the background of the market-place,
stands for the ordinary, well-intentioned person—yet at the eleventh
hour he is still outside the Kingdom.

One notes, too, that he was not without excuse. It is so like our
Lord to touch on that. When the man was asked why he was standing there, he could truly say that nobody had hired him. That this
excuse was not *entirely* valid is, I think, embodied in the parable.
For at the third hour and at the sixth and ninth hours the householder had been out looking for workers. Now had this man been tre-

mendously in earnest, he would have thrown himself in the employer's way; but there is not a hint that he did that. Probably at nine o'clock he was abed; men out of work are prone to oversleep. At twelve o'clock he would be having dinner and at three enjoying his *siesta*. But the beautiful thing is that, though this be true, the Master sees and is at pains to show us, that this man was not without excuse. There are men outside at the eleventh hour who are utterly without excuse. Deaf to every call, they have resisted the inviting Spirit. But there are others who are different from that, and one of the charming things about our Lord is that He finds room for that suggestion in His story. Such may have sat under a sapless ministry or had the Gospel presented in repellent ways. They may have been plunged, when little more than boys, into dubious or soul-destroying businesses. Someone they loved, who made a great profession, may have proved (long years ago) a whited sepulcher—and at the eleventh hour they are still outside the Kingdom.

Now the wonderfully hopeful thing is this, that this man *was* called at the eleventh hour, for the eleventh hour (as Bible students know) is an hour when nothing ever happens. With the exception of this single parable I am not aware that the eleventh hour is mentioned from the Book of Genesis to Revelation. The third hour is a great hour of Scripture, for then (according to St. Mark) our Lord was crucified. And the sixth and ninth are both great hours of Scripture, and all three are Jewish hours of prayer. But the eleventh hour is an hour unchronicled—it is an hour when nothing ever happens—*and it was just then that this man was called*. Nobody had ever heard of such a thing. Nobody ever expected such a thing. The oldest frequenter of the marketplace had never known anyone called at five o'clock. And yet *that* is what happened in the story, and our blessed Lord would never have told the story if it could not happen now—and to you.

For this employer is an extraordinary person. It is *that* which Jesus is eager to impress on us. Had the employer been thinking of nothing but his grapes, he would never have acted in this amazing fashion. What! to hire men when the working-day is closing and to pay them with an insane extravagance? Whoever heard of a business man like that! Such conduct in an employer is unthinkable. And then our Lord would smile and flash a glance at them and say, "Children, that is exactly what I am driving at, for remember that

My householder is God." "My ways are not your ways, neither are My thoughts your thoughts" (Isa. 55:8). This is an extraordinary householder because God is an extraordinary God, giving His only begotten Son to die for us, waiting and watching and yearning for the prodigal, putting a ring on his hand and shoes upon his feet when in the evening he comes limping home (Luke 15:11–32).

And then this eleventh-hour man got far more than he had ever dreamed of. It was almost incredible, but it was true. The men who came at break of day were bargainers. They began by driving a bargain with the master. They said, "Let us settle the wages question first," and he settled it and gave them what they bargained for. But the eleventh-hour man did not drive a bargain; filled with gratitude, he left things to the Master, and he got more than he had ever dreamed of. *That* is the kind of faith which God delights in, *not* the conditional faith that drives a bargain, *not* the faith that says, "If Thou wilt do so-and-so for me, I will do so-and-so for Thee"; but the faith, born of a wondering gratitude, that leaves all issues in the Master's hands, perfectly certain that His name is Love. Think of the amazement of the eleventh hour man when the whole penny was lying in his hand. "What! all this for me? All this for *me*?" Yes: "eye hath not seen, nor ear heard, neither have entered into the heart of man, the things which God hath prepared for them that love Him" (1 Cor. 2:9).

"I girded thee, though thou hast not known me" (Isaiah 45:5).

51

Unconscious Girding

It was to Cyrus, King of Persia, that these words were addressed. They revealed to him the secret of his life. Cyrus had conquered Babylon and granted liberty to captive Israel. From what motives of policy he acted it is perhaps impossible to say. But here the curtain is lifted for a moment, and back of all the conscious aims of Cyrus we see the conqueror in the hand of God. Cyrus was a pagan. He bowed down to the ancient gods of Persia. He had never known the Lord's name nor worshiped toward His holy temple. Yet all the time, right through his youth and manhood and in his handling of victorious armies, God had been girding him although he never knew it. So are we taught that in every separate life, back of our striving there is a plan of God. We are being trained and disciplined and led when we never know anything about it. There is no chance or accident in life. Things we rebel against are in the ordering. Love and wisdom are girding all the time.

We see that with peculiar clarity in the various biographies of Scripture. Think, for instance, of the life of Joseph. When Joseph was seized and cast into the pit, it must have seemed to him a cruel fate. When he was carried off in slavery to Egypt, it must have looked as if God had quite forgotten him. Yet the hour was coming when in that very place, surrounded by his suppliant brothers, Joseph was to say, "It was not you who brought me hither: it was God" (Gen. 45:8). The pit and the slavery were not in Joseph's plan. To him they were cruel and terrible intrusions. Had he been given liberty of choice he certainly never would have chosen such things. And in every life, in your life and in mine, are things we never should have chosen for ourselves, and the question is, how do we regard them? Do we take up a quarrel against life? Are we angry because *our* plans are shattered? Do we feel as if some blind fury were at work with us? Do we resent such meaningless intrusions? My dear reader, there is a better way—it is the way that all the saints have trod—it is to believe that God is girding us, though we never know anything about it. His plans are larger than our plans. They include the bitter and the sweet. There is room in them for loss and sorrow. They embrace the cross as surely as the crown. And the beautiful thing is that this large ordering is the ordering of a Father's love, so that all things work together *for our good.*

One sees that often in the discipline of childhood which is sometimes so hard to understand. Even an unhappy childhood may be *meant.* I had a friend who had an unhappy childhood. He was checked and repressed at every turn. Where other children were open and communicative, he learned to be secretive and silent. And he told me how terribly bitter was his loneliness, and how he used to envy other children who could pour the tale of every day's adventure into a loving mother's ear. But childhood passed and manhood came, and my friend became eminent in one of the professions. A hundred secrets were entrusted to him, to betray one of which would have been treachery. And then it broke on him with sudden awareness that, in his secretive and silent childhood, God had been girding him when he never knew it. *He* never would have chosen such a childhood. It was the last thing in the world he would have chosen—just as that trouble which laid you aside from work is the last thing in the world *you* would have chosen. But the plans of Love are bigger plans than ours and have room in them for things which we resent as intrusions on our happiness or usefulness. Living faith is universal faith. Living faith embraces everything. Living faith delights in holding *everything* within the circuit of the love of heaven. In disappointments, in accidental happenings, in illnesses, in hours of heartbreak, Love is busy girding all the time.

This strengthening philosophy of life was continually proclaimed by the Lord Jesus. It is bound up with His doctrine of God's fatherhood. A father does not only clothe his children; he prepares them for the years that are to come. He does not alone supply the daily bread; he anticipates and trains for the tomorrow. That is why sometimes he denies things. That is why sometimes he rebukes and checks.

That is why he sends his children to school when the birds are singing and the fields are calling. Such things are hard to "thole"[1] sometimes, and the little folk are tempted to rebel. But such things are in the father's plan, *just because* he is a father. And when Jesus teaches us to say "Our Father," bound up with that is the liberating thought that Love is girding when we never know it.

I write this in the Highlands where many tracks lead across the heather. Knee-deep in heather as the traveler is, it is often difficult to see the track. But when he reaches yonder little hill and looks back over the moor that he has crossed, how easily does he discern the pathway. So here we know in part. We are not really here to understand. We are here to walk by faith and not by sight. We are here to keep on keeping on. And my trust is that when at last we climb the hill where Love has its eternal habitations, we shall look back and see with perfect clarity that *everything* was in the plan of heaven.

---

1. endure

"At the time of the end shall be the vision"
(Dan. 8:17).

52

The Vision at the End

In the larger sense of the word *vision*, this is a deep and universal truth. It is a truth we never should forget. We have vision when we understand a thing, when we penetrate to its significance. We have vision when we see the inward meaning of anything we have to do or suffer. And Scripture, in this Book of Daniel which dwells so much on the timeliness of things, declares to us the appointed time of vision. *Not* when plunged into the thick of life, immersed in multifarious details; *not* when the cross is heavy on the shoulder nor when suffering or sorrow overwhelms us; not then must we expect to see nor think God faithless if we cannot see—*at the time of the end shall be the vision.*

Think how true that is of the Creation as you read the story of it in the Bible. I do not envy the modern type of mind that cannot discover inspiration there. First there is the creation of the world in its endless and exquisite variety. Then living things appear upon the scene in the water, on the land, and in the air. But so far, though there is beauty everywhere, and order, and the dawning of intelligence, the world is still destitute of vision. There is no vision of a creating hand yet on the part of any of the living creatures. Bound in the great whole, they discern nothing of its increasing purpose.

Then, at the very end, comes man, the crown and climax of the whole creation, and we remember the deep words of Daniel. At last there is one who understands, who is something more than part of a long process. There is vision now of a meaning in the universe and of a moral law and of a God. And all this, *not* at the beginning but at the very close of the creation—at the time of the end shall be the vision.

One feels, too, how true that is of Christ when we study the story of His life. It is all beautiful and divinely helpful; but the best wine is kept until the last. Where is it that we get our clearest vision of a love which travels to the uttermost? Where do we see the wonder of a sacrifice that assures the vilest sinner of forgiveness? "God commendeth His love to us (and you must put the accent on the *His*) in that while we were yet sinners, Christ *died* for us" (Rom. 5:8). Or think, again, of the passing of the centuries, and how much in the Lord Christ is still unfathomed. For all the devotion of nineteen hundred years, we seem but to touch the hem of His garment yet. We trust Him, we study Him, we preach Him, and always the deepening feeling in our hearts is that the half has never yet been told. It will take all the experiences of all the saints to know the love of Christ. It will take the evangelization of the world to understand the riches of His grace. When China has been garnered and India with its millions gathered in, when every race has made its contribution to the understanding of the Savior, *then* at the time of the end shall be the vision of the glory and fullness of the Lord.

Again, how very true this is, often, of our friends or dear ones we have lost. One has said, and very wisely said, that our friends are never ours until we have lost them. While they are with us we scarcely understand. They are too near for us to see them perfectly. A trifling thing will mar our vision of them, as a grain of sand will irritate the eye. And life is so full of little things, innocent yet often irritant, that we fail sometimes to recognize the friend who joins us on our Emmaus road. Then comes the end, and everything is different. In the large quietness we see. The little trifling irritants are gone. There are no grains of sand to blind us any more. And that is why often, when a dear one passes, we find the words of Daniel coming back to us—at the time of the end shall be the vision.

Lastly, do not the words apply to our own lives? If you were climbing up some ancient tower, I know not how many steps would be to climb. But suppose there were four hundred steps, then at the three hundredth there would still be darkness. What! after all the weary climbing, darkness and these impenetrable walls? Yes, *it is the last step that gives the vision.*

So, I take it, is it with our life here. We climb, and very often it is dark. We cannot recognize eternal purposes. We fail to see the love of God in things. But if we hold to it and keep on climbing, even though heart and flesh should fail occasionally, we shall discover just as Daniel did, that at the time of the end shall be the vision.

"He took upon Him the form of a servant"
(Phil. 2:7).

53

The Form of a Servant

On one occasion our Lord announced, "I am among you as one who serveth." That was the summation of His ministry. The word for *serveth* which St. John gives us is a word of very large and liberal meaning. It includes services of every kind, however high or exalted they may be. But when St. Paul says of that same Lord that He took on Him the form of a servant, *that* is an entirely different word. It is the common term for slave or, as we might put it, for domestic servant. There was nothing of lofty ministry about it; it was colored with contemptuous suggestion. Paul was thinking of his home in Tarsus where, unregarded and unthanked, the slaves were busy in menial occupations. No one knew better than the great apostle that life in its last analysis is service. The Grecian statesman and the Roman general were the servants of commonwealth or empire. But what awed Paul when he thought of Christ was *not* that He was found in such a category. It was that He humbled Himself to the likeness of a slave.

There is a service which is highly honorable. It is compatible with great position. I have a postcard I once got from Mr. Gladstone,[1] and it is signed "Your obedient servant." But the slave's

---

1. William Gladstone (1809–1898), British statesman and prime minister.

service was of another order, quite apart from honorable ministries, and in *that* lay the wonder of the Lord. The slave legally had no possessions, and *He* had not where to lay His head. No freeman acknowledged a slave in public places, and from *Him* men hid, as it were, their faces. The slave was universally despised, and his master could maltreat him as he pleased. And *He* was despised of men and, being maltreated, opened not His mouth.

This aspect of the Lord's obedience constitutes the wonder of His childhood. It explains, as it illuminates, the strange silence of the gospel story. There are apocryphal gospels of the infancy that credit the little Boy with various miracles. He strikes a comrade who instantly falls dead; He makes clay sparrows, and they fly away. But the real wonder of the childhood does not lie in miracles like these but in *this*, that even in His boyhood He took on Him the form of a servant. Did Mary never ask Him of a morning to go and fetch the water from the well? Did she never say, "Child, I'm very tired today, will you run to the village shop and do an errand?" And the beautiful way in which He did such biddings was a far more wonderful thing to seeing eyes than any reported miracles on sparrows. He, the eternal Son of God, running little errands for His mother; He, who might have grasped equality with God, lighting the cottage fire and fetching water—*that* was the astounding thing to Paul, as it was to all of the evangelists, as is so clear from their majestic silence.

Or, again, we think of these long years when He was the Carpenter of Nazareth. And once again legend has been busy seeking to give content to these years. Strange stories soon grew current of amazing things that had happened in that workshop. Beams had been miraculously lengthened, and plows, in a moment, miraculously made. But to all this, in the inspired evangelists there is not even a reference in passing. For *them* the abiding wonder lay elsewhere. Do any of my readers keep a shop? Don't *they* know how hard it is to serve their customers? Aren't some of these customers very hard to please and often irritating and unreasonable? And one may be certain if it be so in Britain where at least the atmosphere is Christian, it would be worse in uneducated Nazareth. The Carpenter was at the beck and call of everybody. There was no pleasing some of the folk in Nazareth. It was a thankless and often humiliating service, that of a carpenter in a provincial village. And to Paul the

wonder of these years was not the miraculous lengthening of beams.
It was the stooping to a drudgery like that. In the beginning was the
Word, and the Word was with God, and the Word was God (John
1:1). Christ was the brightness of His Father's glory and the express
image of His person (Heb. 1:3). And then Paul thought of the
carpenter's shop at Nazareth, with its exacting and uneducated customers, and wrote, *He took on Him the form of a servant.*

In the public ministry, again, there is one incident which illuminates our text. It is an hour the world will not willingly let die. In
the East it was one of the duties of the slave to wash the feet of the
arriving traveler, for men wore only sandals then, and the highways
(save in rain) were very dusty. And Peter, at any rate, never could
forget how once, and very near the end, the Master had done that
office of the slave. Would he not be certain to tell that to Paul when
they talked together as we know from the Acts they did? Would not
Peter enact it and draw back his feet to show Paul what had actually
happened? Perhaps it was then there flashed into Paul's mind the
magnificent daring of our text, coupling the Lord of heaven with a
menial. Jesus, knowing that He was come from God and went to
God, girded Himself and washed the disciples' feet. He did it, *not*
forgetting His divinity. He did it because He knew He was divine.
Brooding on which, Paul took his pen and wrote, "Who being in the
form of God, *took on Him the form of a servant.*"

"Things present" (Rom. 8:38).

54
The Separating Power of Things Present

It is notable that in his enumeration of things which might dim the love of God to us, the apostle should make mention of things present, and by things present I take it that he means the events and trials of the present day. Many of us know how things to come may tempt us to doubt the love of God. The anxieties and forebodings of tomorrow often cloud the sunshine of today. But Paul, who knew all that as well as we do for his apostleship gave no exemptions, knew also the separating power of things present. The task in which we are presently engaged, the thronging duties of the common day, the multitude of things we must get through before we betake ourselves to bed at night, these, unless we continually watch, are apt to blind us to the great realities and to separate us from the love of God in Christ.

In part that separating power arises from the exceeding nearness of things present. Things which are very near command our vision and often lead to erroneous perspective. When I light the lamp in my quiet study, the moon may be riding through the sky, the stars may be glittering in heavenly brilliance, proclaiming that the hand which made them is divine. But the lamp is near me at my side, and

I read by it and write my letters by it, and very often the stars are quite forgotten. Things present are things near, and near things have a certain blinding power. You can blot the sun out with a halfpenny piece if you only hold it near enough the eye. And yet the sun is a majestic creature, beautifier and conserver of the world, and the halfpenny is but a worn and trifling coin. For most of us each day that dawns brings its round of present duties. They absorb us, commanding every energy, and so doing may occasionally blind us. And that is why in busy crowded lives where near things are so swift to tyrannize, we all require moments of withdrawal. To halt a moment and just to say "God loves me"; to halt a moment and say "God is here"; to take the halfpenny from the eye an instant that we may see the wonder of the sun; that, as the apostle knew so well, is one of the secrets of the saints, to master the separating power of things present.

Another element in that separating power is the difficulty of understanding present things. It is always easier to understand our yesterdays than to grasp the meaning of today. Often in the Highlands it is difficult to see the path just at one's feet. Any bunch of cowberries may hide it, or any bush of over-arching heather. But when one halts a moment and looks back, generally it is comparatively easy to trace the path as it winds across the moor. So we begin to understand our past, its trials, its disappointments, and its illnesses; but such things are very hard to understand in their actual moment of occurrence, and it is *that*, the difficulty of reading love in the dark characters of present things, which constitutes their separating power. Many a grown man thanks God for the discipline of early childhood. But as a child it was often quite unfathomable, and he doubted if his mother loved him. And we are all God's children, never in love with the discipline of love, and in that lies the separating power of things present.

Another element of that separating power is found in the distraction of things present. "Life isn't a little bundle of big things: it's a big bundle of little things." I read somewhere of a ship-captain who reported that a lighthouse was not shining. Inquiries were made, and it was found that the light was burning brightly all the night. What dimmed the light and made it as though it were not, to the straining eyes of the captain on the bridge, was a cloud of myriads of little flies. "While thy servant was busy here and there, the man was gone." What things escape us in our unending busyness! Peace and joy and the power of self-control and the serenity that ought to mark the Christian. And sometimes *that* is lost, which to lose is the tragedy of tragedies—the sense and certainty of love divine. Preoccupied, it fades out of our heaven. The comfort and the calm of it are gone. The light is there "forever, ever shining," but the cloud of flies has blotted out the light. Nobody knew better than the apostle did, in the cares that came upon him daily, the separating power of things present.

Of spiritual victory over present things, the one perfect example is our Lord. It is He who affords to us a perfect picture of untiring labor and unruffled calm. He gained the conquest over things to come. When Calvary was coming He was joyous. He set His face steadily toward Jerusalem where the bitter Cross was waiting Him. But, wonderful though that victory was over everything the future had in store, there was another that was not less wonderful. Never doubting the love of God to Him, certain of it in His darkest hour, through broken days, through never-ending calls, when there was not leisure so much as to eat, not only did He master things to come, but He did what is often far more difficult—He mastered the separating power of things present. Do not forget He did all that for us. His victories were all achieved for us. In a deep sense we do not win our victories—we appropriate the victories of Christ. That is why the apostle in another place says, "All things are yours—*things present*, things to come—for ye are Christ's, and Christ is God's" (1 Cor. 3:22–23).

"What time I am afraid, I will trust in Thee" (Ps. 56:3).

55

fear and faith

Let us consider for a little while some of the springs of human fear, and first, note how many of our fears spring from *the imagination*. It has been said (and I think truly said) that life is ruled by the imagination. The things we picture and weave in glowing colors have a very powerful influence over conduct. Often that influence is stimulative, illumining the pathway to discovery; often it creates or liberates fear. People who are highly sensitive are far more apt to be fearful than their neighbors. There are a hundred fears that never touch the man of stolid, unimaginative nature. That is why for a certain type of person to be brave may be comparatively easy and for another, infinitely hard.

Now, the worst thing about this kind of fear is that reason is powerless to allay it. You might as soon allay a fire with good advice. Argument is cold. It cannot banish the specters of the soul. It has no brush that can obliterate the pictures of the imagination. But there is another way, more powerful than reason, to overcome imaginative fears, and that is the way of this inspired psalmist. Faith is the antidote to fear. It quiets fear as the mother quiets her child. The child still dreams, but the dreams are not reality. It is the mother's arms that are reality. So we, His children, dreaming in the darkness and sometimes very frightened by our dreams, find "underneath the everlasting arms" (Deut. 33:27).

Another very common source of fear is *weakness or frailty of body*. Every one is familiar with that. When we are strong and well it is not difficult to keep our fears at bay. Fears, like microbes, do not love the sunshine. They need the darkness for their propagation. That is why, when the lights of life are dim, we readily become the prey of fearfulness. Burdens we can bear without a thought when we are strong and vigorous and well, tasks we can meet with quiet equal hearts, difficulties we can bravely face, these seem insurmountable when we are worn and often plunge us into the lowest pit. We must never forget how the temper of the mind is affected by the condition of the body. Health is not alone the source of happiness. It is one of the perennial springs of hope. Many of our vague uncharted fears, which haunt us and rob us of the sunshine, are rooted in the frailty of our frame.

Now I have no doubt that many of my readers are far from being physically perfect. The fact is, there are very few of us who could be described as physically perfect. And to all such, whatever their condition, I want to give these noble words of Scripture: "What time I am afraid, I will trust in Thee." He knows our frame. He remembers we are dust. He made us and He understands us. He alone can perfectly appreciate the interactions of body and of mind. And when we trust Him in a childlike faith, nothing is more evident in life than the way in which He disappoints our fears. His grace is sufficient for us. Often when we are weak, then are we strong. Drawing from Him we find we have our fullness, given us daily as the manna was, until at last the "body of our humiliation" shall be fashioned like His glorious body, and then such fears will be laid to rest forever.

I close by naming one other source of fear, and that is the *faculty of conscience*. A guilty conscience is a fearing conscience—conscience does make cowards of us all. Could we get rid of conscience, what fears would go whistling down the wind! But God has so created us, that *that* is the one thing we cannot do. We may drug and dope it, we may silence it, we may sear it as with an iron, but, like the maiden, it is not dead but sleeping. It awakens in unexpected seasons, sometimes in the stillness of the night, or when our loved ones are removed in death, or when we see our sins bearing fruit in others—perhaps most often in our dying hours, when the flaming colors of time no longer blind us, and we draw near to the revealings of eternity. All the fears of our imagination, all the fears that spring from weakly bodies, all these, however haunting, are nothing to the fears of conscience. And the tremendous fact, never to be denied by any theory of its evolution, is that God has put conscience in the breast.

But He who has put conscience in the breast has done something more wonderful than that. To minister relief to fearing conscience, He has put His Only-begotten on the tree. There, explain it how you will, is freedom from the hideous fears of conscience. There, explain it how you will, is release from the terrors of our guilt. One trustful look at the Lord Jesus Christ dying upon the Cross of Calvary, and the fearfulness of conscience is no more. There is now therefore no more condemnation (Rom. 8:1). Pardoned, we have joy and peace. God is *for* us on the Cross, and if God be for us, who can be against us? (Rom. 8:31). Blessed Savior who did die for us and whose blood cleanses from all sin, *What time I am afraid, I will trust in Thee.*

"There cometh a woman of Samaria to draw water" (John 4:7).

56

The Casual Contacts of Jesus

One notes in the life of Jesus how many folk there were who met Him casually. The meetings were in no sense prearranged; they were unplanned and unpremeditated contacts. One may hold that in the deepest senses no meeting with the Lord is really casual. Contingencies are not outside the will of Heaven. Still, speaking in the way of men, no one can read the life of Jesus without observing how very full it was of what we call casual encounters. The woman of Samaria had no idea that she was going to meet the Lord beside the well. It was with no thought that he would meet with Christ that the man with the withered hand went to the synagogue (Mark 3:1). The impotent man beside the pool was not waiting for Him who is our Peace—he was waiting for the troubling of the waters (John 5:1–9). All these were casual meetings, speaking in the common parlance of men. They did not issue from definite intention as in the case of the Greeks who sought an interview (John 12:20–21). And how our Lord comported Himself, in what we may call these casual encounters, is a deeply interesting study.

One might be sure, from all we know of life, that such meetings would be rich in consequence; doubly sure when we remember the radiant personality of Jesus. Mark Rutherford,[1] in "Miriam's Schooling," tells us of a man who was now growing old. That man, when twenty years of age, had one day passed a woman in the street. And the spiritual beauty of her face, he tells us, haunted him and held him to the end. A thousand times it had rebuked him, and a thousand times it had redeemed him. Not infrequently, when we are dull or troubled, we meet someone in the most casual fashion, and instantly (such is personality) the time of the singing of the birds has come. Now multiply all that by the radiant personality of Jesus, and you grasp the consequence of casual contact. Life was going to be different forever to that Samaritan woman by the well. There was going to be work and happiness at home for the man with the withered hand. Yet these were but casual meetings—momentary encounters by the way—unpremeditated and unplanned. There is a line in a well-known hymn which says, "Not a brief glimpse I beg, a passing word." One understands that perfectly. It is love demanding the *forever*. But do not forget that a passing word of Christ—a single glimpse of the beauty of His face may alter life down to its very depths and make the future different forever.

It is a beautiful and helpful thought that for these casual meetings Christ always had time, and the wonder of that deepens when one recalls the greatness of His mission. His was the most stupendous mission ever given to a son of man. He was here to bear the sins of the whole world. He was here to make all things new. It is when one thinks of that, and the weight and pressure of it, and the brief years allowed for its accomplishment, that one marvels at the leisurely serenity with which He took these casual encounters. With a baptism to be baptized with, living under the urgency of Calvary, who could have wondered had He been preoccupied, pushing aside every casual comer? Yet He had time to halt when Bartimæus cried (Mark 10:46), and to sit and talk with the woman at the well, and to wait serenely until they discovered her who had gripped the tassel of His garment (Matt. 9:20). That is often a very comforting thought when we come to Him upon the throne today. With the government upon His shoulder, can I reasonably hope He will have time for *me*?

---

1. Pseudonym for W. H. White (1831–1931), English writer.

Yet on earth He always had the time and the heart at leisure from itself—and He is the same yesterday, today, and forever.

One likes to think, too, how in these casual meetings our Lord gave of His very best, and He did that because He gave Himself. It is a thought familiar in many a book and sermon that Jesus gave of His best to the *one*. That is profoundly true, as every reader of the gospel knows. But still more striking and suggestive is it that He gave of His best to the *casual one*. I could understand Him dealing with Nicodemus so, for Nicodemus deliberately sought Him (John 3:1). He took his courage in both hands and braved a deal when he set out to meet the Lord that night. But that Jesus should give of His richest and His best to folk who met Him in quite casual contact— that is the kind of thing which gives one pause. He did that with the woman at the well. The words He spoke to her have changed the world. They have come ringing down the corridors of time, nor will men ever let them die. Yet she went out that noonday just to fill her waterpot, at an hour when she might hope to be alone, without one thought that she would meet the Lord.

Now may I say quietly to all my readers that *there* He has left us an example. Sometimes going into company we say, "I must be at my very best tonight." And sometimes preachers, addressing certain audiences, say, "I must be at my very best today." But who can tell the good that we might do, who explore the influence we might wield, if we only determined to give of our very best in the casual contacts of the hour? There may be a bit of the Kingdom in a handshake and a gleam of heaven in a happy smile. A word of cheer to some poor "down and out" may be as a well of water in a thirsty land. That, I take it, was the Master's way, and if in joy and peace it be our way, casual folk will be thanking God for us, though we never hear anything about it.

"Thou hast made. . . winter" (Ps. 74:17).

57

The Higher Offices of Winter

It is always easy to believe that God has made the summer-time. There is something in a perfect summer day that speaks to us of the divine. The beauty which is around us everywhere, the singing of the birds in every tree, the warmth of the pleasant summer sun, the amazing prodigality of life, these, as by filaments invisible, draw our hearts to the Giver of them all and make it easy to say, "Thou hast made the summer." With winter it is different. It is not so easy to see the love of God there. There is a great deal of suffering in winter, both for the animal creation and for man. It may therefore aid the faith of some who may be tempted to doubt the love of God in winter if I suggest some of its spiritual offices.

One of the higher offices of winter is to deepen our appreciation of the summer. We should be blind if summer were perpetual. Someone has said, and very truly said, that our dear ones are only ours when we have lost them. They have to pass away into the silent land before we know them for what they really are. And in like manner summer has to pass, leaving us in the grip of icy winter, before we fully appreciate the summer. It is not the man who lives in bonnie Scotland who feels most deeply how beautiful Scotland is. It is the exile on some distant shore yearning for the mountains and the glens. It is not the man with rude unbroken

185

health who feels most deeply the value of his health. *That* is realized when health is shattered. In Caithness, where I lived four years, there is a great scarcity of trees. I never knew how much I loved the trees until I dwelt in a land where there are none. And we never know all that summer means to us in its pageantry of life and beauty until we lose it in the barrenness of winter. Lands that have no winter have no spring. They never know the thrilling of the spring—when the primroses awake and the wild hyacinths and the "livelier iris" changes on the dove. Thoughts like these in January days make it easier for faith to say, "*Thou* hast made the winter."

Another of the higher offices of winter is the larger demands it makes upon the will. I should like to take a simple illustration. In summer it is comparatively easy to get out of bed at the appointed hour, for the earth is warm, and the birds are busy singing, and the light is streaming through the open windows. But in winter, to fling the covers off and get up when it is dark and perishingly cold, *that* is quite a different affair. That calls for a certain resolution. It makes instant demands upon the will. Now broaden that thought to the compass of the day, and you reach a truth that cannot be denied. The countries where the will is most developed and where moral life is most vigorous and strong are the countries that have winter in their year. There "ain't no ten commandments east of Suez," says Kipling in a familiar line.[1] The singular thing is that east of Suez there isn't any winter in the year. Rigorous winter days, when life is difficult and when it takes some doing even to get up, are God's tonic for His children's will. "O well for him whose will is strong. He suffers, but he does not suffer long."[2] Let any young fellow have his will at heel, and he is on the highway to his victory. Summer is languid; winter makes us resolute. We have to do things when we don't feel like them. And Thou—the Giver of the ten commandments—*Thou* hast made the winter.

Another of the high offices of winter is to intensify the thought of home. In lands that bask in a perpetual sunshine, home-life is always at a minimum. I had a friend who for three years was prisoner in an internment camp in Germany. I asked him once when he felt most homesick, and his answer I am not likely to forget. He

---

1. From "Mandalay" by Rudyard Ripling (1865–1936), English poet.
2. From "Will" by Tennyson.

said that the only times when he felt homesick were when fog settled down upon the camp, reminding him of winter-fogs in Glasgow. In summer he was happy. It was good to be alive in summer. But when the fog came, he thought of lighted streets and saw his cozy and comfortable home. And always the thought of home is sweetest, and the home-life richest and most beautiful, in the dark, cold season of the winter. We talk in the same breath of hearth and home, and it is in winter that the hearth is glowing. There is one poem about a humble home more beautiful than any other in our literature. It is a picture by the hand of genius of the joy and reverence of the hearth. But the "Cottar's Saturday Night"[3] could never have been written in the tropics. It is the child of a land with winter in its year. Now think of everything we owe to home. Think of what the nation owes to home. "From scenes like these auld Scotia's grandeur springs."[4] Home is the basis of national morality. Is it not easier when one thinks of these things to say in the bitterest January day, *"Thou* hast made the winter"?

The last office of winter I shall mention is how it stirs our sluggish hearts to charity. With that we are all perfectly familiar. Did you ever watch a singer in the street in the warm and balmy days of summer? The passers-by pay him little heed though he be singing all the charms of "Annie Laurie." But in winter, when the air is biting and when the snow is deep upon the ground, "Annie Laurie" brings him in a harvest. Folk are extraordinarily good to me in giving me donations for the poor. For one donation that I get in summer-time, I get ten in the bitterness of winter. Winter unlocks the gates of charity. It unseals the hidden springs of pity. It moves us with compassion for the destitute, and so to be moved is a very Christlike thing. Such thoughts as these in stern and icy days, when we are tempted perhaps to doubt the love of God, make it easier to say with David, *"Thou* hast made the winter."

---

3. By Robert Burns (1786).
4. Ibid.

"Art Thou He that should come, or do we
look for another?" (Matt. 11:3).

58

Do We Look for Another?

I wish to say a few words on the finality of our Christian faith, and
there could be no better approach to that than the experience of
John the Baptist. When John cried "Behold the Lamb of God"
(John 1:36) he was asserting the finality of Christ. All the lambs
slain on Jewish altars were but prophecies and presages of Christ.
He was the completion and the crown of the long and chequered
history of Israel, and beyond Him there could never be another.
Then doubts began to assail the mind of John. All was so contrary
to expectation. This lowly Savior, moving about the villages, was
so different from the Messiah of his dreams. And then, as in a
torturing agony, John sent his disciples to the Lord, saying, "Art
Thou He that should come, or do we look for another?"

Now that question, if I am not mistaken, is in many earnest
minds today. Many are asking, secretly or openly, if Christ be the
final Word of God. Partly through the comparative study of religions with its appreciation of what is beautiful in all, partly through
the slowness of our faith to bring the Kingdom into our teeming
cities, partly through the supineness of the Church in answering the
challenge of our social problems, that question is being widely
asked today. Is Christ the final Word of God? Is a new world-

teacher still to be revealed? Or, in the abstract language of the West, is our Christian faith the final faith? That is being discussed more widely than many of the orthodox imagine.

That our faith (like polytheism) will die a natural death is a thought that may be at once rejected. Heaven and earth *have* passed away, and His word has not passed away. Much more conceivable is the thought of certain circles that our Christian faith will be absorbed in some synthesis of what is best in all religions. That, we are told, is what has happened with Judaism. All that is best in it was absorbed in Christianity—its sense of guilt, its craving for atonement, its profound sense of the holiness of God. And if this has been the fate of Judaism, itself one of the revealed religions, may it not be so with that which has replaced it? But there is this profound difference to be noted—Judaism could never satisfy. Paul, who embraced it with passionate intensity, found himself thirsty and hungry at the end. Whereas the wonderful thing about our faith is this, that, take it where you will throughout the world, it absolutely satisfies the heart. Take it to India, and that is true. Take it to Africa, and that is true. Take it to the cultured or the ignorant, and when they find its secret, that is true. Paul needed Judaism *and something else* if he was to win perfect satisfaction. Nobody needs Christ and something else. That infinite satisfaction which our faith gives, that profound sense of being complete in Christ, that song which rises from the believing heart, "Thou, O Christ, art all I want," *that* distinguishes our faith decisively from Judaism and every other faith. It is the mark of its absolute finality.

To some this may seem a theoretic question, but in reality it is far from being that. For example, unless our faith be final it cannot demand unconditional surrender—and that is exactly what it *does* demand. No one would cast himself upon another if he knew that the other's friendship were but temporary. Love demands finality if it is to give itself in utter unreserve. And the utter unreserve our faith demands could not be asked, and never could be given, were our faith destined to be superseded. Religion is nothing unless it can be everything, unless it deserves unconditional surrender, unless we can rest ourselves upon it unreservedly in life and trial and suffering and death. And that is what nobody can ever do, any more than he can give his love or friendship, if what claims his heart is only temporary.

Again, one remembers that our Christian faith is in its essence a missionary faith. Whenever it ceases to be that, it ceases to be Christianity. From the first it has evangelized the world simply because it could not help it. It could no more help it than the river can help flowing, or the rain, coming down on the mown grass. But the instant you cease to believe our faith is final and that Christ is the last Word of God, you "cut the nerve" of missionary effort.

To what purpose is this waste—this lavish expenditure of men and money—if the message of the Cross is to grow obsolete and Christ be replaced by any other teacher? Do you think our Lord, who was always sweetly reasonable, would ever have said, "Go into all the world" (Matt. 28:19–20), had He foreseen a prospect such as that? The genius of Christianity is missionary, and all missionaries believe that Christ is final. Men who hold Him one teacher among many have never lifted a finger to evangelize the nations. Thus this question, seemingly theoretic, has the mightiest influence on personal response and on the coming of the Kingdom in the world.

And then we remember how right through the New Testament that is the unvarying attitude—and when we cut ourselves adrift from the New Testament, we are sailing on an uncharted sea. Paul never doubted that his faith was final through all the magnificent expansions of his thought. To John, Christ was the Alpha and the Omega, the beginning and the end. The majestic argument of the Epistle to the Hebrews is an argument for the finality of Christ—God has at last spoken by a Son. Best of all, our Savior never doubted it—it was part and parcel of His consciousness. I am the Bread of Life (John 6:35). I am the Light of the World (John 8:12). My words shall never pass away (Luke 21:33). No one has had even a glimpse of Christianity who cannot sing with the profoundest faith—

> Jesus shall reign where'er the sun
> Doth his successive journeys run.[1]

---

1. From "Jesus Shall Reign" by Isaac Watts (1674–1748).

"Thou hast been faithful over a few things"
(Matt. 25:21).

59

The Lowly Duty of Fidelity

It was very like our Lord to make fidelity the test of life. He was quick to recognize the lowly virtues. Just as He took obscure and lowly men when He wanted to build up a kingdom, so did He take obscure and lowly virtues when He wanted to build up a character, and this not merely because they *were* obscure, but because they were within the range of all, and His was to be a universal gospel. There is nothing dazzling in fidelity. It is not at all a rare and splendid gift. It has no power to arrest the eyes nor get itself chronicled in any newspaper. And it is singularly like the Lord, with His passion for undistinguished people, that He should crown a virtue such as that. Some of my readers never can be brilliant. They serve in the great army of the commonplace. But there is one thing within the compass of them all, and *that* is the steady practice of fidelity. And the inspiring thought is that our Lord should take a thing within the reach of everybody and make it the criterion of character.

It is like Him, too, to recognize that fidelity demands a certain courage. In the parable from which our text is taken that is very charmingly exhibited. There is one man there who was not faithful. He took his talent and he buried it. And it is a master-touch of a profound psychology that in the end of the day, when the reckoning

191

was taken, that man is made to say *I was afraid*. His infidelity was fear, and the Lord delights to hint at truth by negatives. There is a courage of the battlefield which is often a very splendid thing. There is a courage needed for every high adventure, whether it be in Africa or Everest. But perhaps the finest courage in the world (in the eyes of God, if not of men) is the quiet and steady courage of fidelity. To do things when you don't feel like them, to keep on keeping on, to get to duty through headache and through heartache, to ply the drudgery when birds are calling—there are few things finer in the world. That is not a thing of the rare moment—it is carrying victory into the common day. It does not flash in the country of our dreams—it illuminates the dreary levels. And life is never a victorious business unless our common days are full of victories of which no one ever hears anything at all.

I should like to halt a moment that I might say in passing that this was the courage of our Lord Himself. Sometimes we forget how brave He was. We sing of "Gentle Jesus, meek and mild," and we dwell on His exceeding tenderness; and in a world like this, so full of difficulty, we can never dwell on His tenderness too much. But if we ignore His courage, we lose one of the appeals of Christ to youth, and to do *that* is infinitely pitiful. Did it take no courage to come down from heaven and become the tenant of a cottage? Did it take no courage to remain at Nazareth when His heart was burning in His breast? Did it take no courage to resist the devil, offering Him the kingdoms of the world, when the winning of these kingdoms was His passion? To scorn delights and live laborious days, to take the long, long trail that led to Calvary, to set His face steadfastly toward Jerusalem where the Cross was waiting and the crown of thorns—never was finer courage in the world. When we feel that we are missing things (and to feel *that* means an aching heart), when we are tempted to rebel at drudgery and to long for the wings of a dove to fly away, we must remember Him who never flew away (though white-winged angels were His servitors), but took up His cross, daily, to the end.

Another profound suggestion of our Lord is that fidelity is rewarded by capacity. "Thou hast been faithful over a few things, I will make thee ruler over many things." Sometimes an employer of labor says to me, "The young fellow you sent me is no use. He has proved a slacker in his task, and I never can offer him a bigger one." But sometimes he says to me. "I've been watching that lad; he's doing splendidly; the first bigger thing that offers he will get." The real reward is not the bigger task. It is the capacity to do the bigger task. Real rewards are never arbitrary; they are vitally related to the toil. The reward of service is greater power to serve. The reward of fidelity is new capacity—added fitness comes through being faithful. To be faithful in the least is to be qualifying for what is greater. To do with the whole heart the lowliest thing is to be getting ready for the higher thing. So live, and whatever the world may have in store, He whose word can never pass away will make you ruler over many things. Life will deepen and be enriched for you, though your home be but a humble lodging. Your will shall be strengthened by those daily victories which, after all, are the victories that count. True wealth is augmented personality with corresponding increase of capacity, and the avenue of God to that is faithfulness.

We shall not forget, in closing let me say, how our Lord associates fidelity with joy. "Enter thou into the joy of thy Lord" (Matt. 25:21). Tell me, is not that profoundly true? Here are two men engaged at the same task, both intelligent and skillful workmen. But the one is careless, and he scamps[1] his work; the other is laboriously faithful. At the end of the day when work is over and there stretches ahead the leisure of the evening, which of these two workmen is the happier? "Flowers laugh before thee in their beds," says Wordsworth[2] of the man who is found faithful. Unfaithfulness moves toward the dark. Fidelity pitches its tent toward the sunrise. Only be faithful, and when the task is over and the morning breaks upon the farther shore, you shall enter into the joy of your Lord.

---

1. to be negligent
2. From "Ode to Duty."

"Thou didst cleave the earth with rivers"
(Hab. 3:9).

60

The Ministry of Division

A little knowledge of geology tells us that this is literally true.
Not even the earthquake divides the earth so surely as does the
ceaseless flowing of the river. It may be a river of water or that
strange river of ice we call a glacier; it may be nothing but a
Highland brook, brawling and brattling down the mountainside; yet
that tide, flowing through the centuries, will work far more effectu-
ally than dynamite in splitting the smooth surface of the earth. That
fact was familiar to this poet, and here he employs it in a very
beautiful way. For to him the rent and riven earth was a token of the
anger of the Highest. And then in the very midst of that hot anger
he sees the glimmerings of heavenly mercy, for "Thou splittest the
earth *with rivers*." In Scripture the river is always a blessed thing. It
makes glad the city of our God. Everything lives wherever the river
comes. It is the symbol of joy and the secret of fertility. All this
hints to us in true poetic fashion that God has beautiful purposes to
serve in His strange and constant ministry of division.

Now if that ministry is evident in nature, it is also evident in
human life. Life is not a vast and endless level—it is cleft just like
the surface of the world. The mystics tell us that time is not divided.
It is a motionless and everlasting present. But it is not thus that God

in His great mercy mediates time to His weak and struggling children. He divides it not that He may conquer; He divides it that we may conquer. He cleaves it as He cleaves the earth with rivers. Time *for us* is split into day and night with recurring hours of labor and of sleep. It is split into the cycles of the weeks, each week opening with its day of rest. It is split by illnesses and tragic happenings and interruptions of our level days. It is split by the coming of New Year. Then there leaps on us the thought of this fine poet, "Thou cleavest the earth *with rivers.*" All these divisions are big with mercy. They are divinely used for gladness and fertility. One of God's great ministries of love is the recurrent ministry of division.

One thinks, for instance, how amazingly it helps to make life an interesting thing. The fact is that an undivided life would be very much like an undivided book. If you had a book of four or five hundred pages that ran on without a single stop, however fascinating the contents were, that book would be extraordinarily hard to read. It is the dividing of what is really one—the dividing into paragraphs and chapters—that helps to sustain interest to the end. Every writer knows those editors who will insist on dividing up his manuscript. The editor's aim is to keep the interest fresh, and knowing his readers, he divides. And it seems to me (and I speak with the utmost reverence) that God is not unlike these editors with that strange manuscript we call our life. If time ran on without one single division, what a dreary business life would be. We should grow tired of it long before the end. We should heartily wish that it were over. But the new morning comes, and the new week begins, and the New Year is ringing on the bells, and we are allured and fascinated to the finish. We grow weary of the unbroken prairie. We never grow weary of the Scottish Highlands where the glens are, and the corries[1] in the hills, and the gullies where the brook is singing. Alike in the world of nature and of life, God interests and captivates His children by the beautiful ministry of division.

Again one thinks how this same ministry checks the momentum of what is bad in us. That is perhaps especially apparent in the division of time into day and night. Many a day, beginning with the sunshine, is dull and dreary by the afternoon. And often in the interior life, there comes a change like that upon ourselves. We

---

1. a circular mountain hollow

196 Highways of the Heart

grow weary; we cease to be alert; our wills lose some of their power of resistance; unworthy things creep into our life. If *that* went on unbroken, what hope would there be for any one of us? All that is bad in us would gain momentum until at last it might be irresistible.

One of God's great ways of rescuing us and of saving us from our unworthier selves is the divine ministry of division. Night comes. We fall asleep. We are released from the pressure of ourselves. The momentum of what is bad in us is broken by the resistless hand of our unconscious hours. And then the morning dawns, and it is another day, and our vision is clearer, and our will is stronger in the interrupting providence of God. "Thou splittest the earth *with rivers.*" There is heavenly loving-kindness in these divisions. They unlock the grip—they shatter the continuity of evil. That is the value of every new day, and that is the value of the Sabbath Day. The Sabbath was made for man.

This beautiful ministry of divisions, too, helps us to begin again. For as Dr. Whyte[2] used to impress on me, the perseverance of the saints consists in new beginnings. The victor is not the man who never stumbles. "Life, like war, is a series of mistakes." The victor is he who after every overthrow has the quiet courage to begin again. And the fine thing about God's ministry of division is the recurring opportunities it offers us for starting again with our faces toward the sunrise. If time for us were an unbroken thing, it might be incredibly hard to start again. But time *for us* (whatever it be for God) is divided as the earth is divided with rivers. And every new morning and every new week and perhaps especially every New Year is God's allurement to a new beginning. Will any of my readers take that to heart? Some of them have made a sorry mess of things. But the perseverance of the saints is not continuous; their perseverance consists of new beginnings. "In the beginning—God" (Gen. 1:1). So let them use the division of New Year. He divides the earth—*with rivers,* and the river of God is full of water.

---

2. Alexander Whyte (1837–1921), Free Church of Scotland clergyman.

Scripture Index

Sermon Resources
by Warren W. Wiersbe

Treasury of the World's Great Sermons
These outstanding sermons are presented from 122 of the greatest preachers. A short biographical sketch of every preacher is also included. Complete with an index of texts and of sermons. 672 double-column pp.

ISBN 0-8254-4002-5　　　　　　　**672 pp.**　　　　　　　**paperback**

Classic Sermons on the Attributes of God
These classic sermons lay a solid foundation for the study of God's attributes such as truth, holiness, sovereignty, omnipresence, immutability, and love. Includes messages by Henry Ward Beecher, J.D. Jones, J.H. Jowett, D.L. Moody, John Wesley, and others.

ISBN 0-8254-4038-6　　　　　　　**160 pp.**　　　　　　　**paperback**

Classic Sermons on the Birth of Christ
The central theme of the Bible is expanded and expounded in this collection of sermons from such great preachers as Henry P. Liddon, Walter A. Maier, G. Campbell Morgan, Arthur T. Pierson, James S. Stewart and others.

ISBN 0-8254-4044-0　　　　　　　**160 pp.**　　　　　　　**paperback**

Classic Sermons on Christian Service
Dynamic principles for Christian service will be found in these classic sermons by highly acclaimed pulpit masters. Warren W. Wiersbe has carefully selected sermons which describe the essential characteristics of Christian servanthood.

ISBN 0-8254-4041-6　　　　　　　**160 pp.**　　　　　　　**paperback**

Classic Sermons on the Cross of Christ
An inspiring collection of sermons on perhaps the most significant event the world ever experienced—the cross of Christ. Through masterful sermons by great pulpit masters, the reader will gain a greater understanding of the theological, devotional, and practical importance of the Cross of Christ.

ISBN 0-8254-4040-8　　　　　　　**160 pp.**　　　　　　　**paperback**

Classic Sermons on Faith and Doubt
A collection of 12 carefully selected sermons, the goal of which is to stimulate the growth and maturity of the believer's faith. Among the preachers represented are: A. C. Dixon, J. H. Jowett, D. Martyn Lloyd-Jones, G. Campbell Morgan, and Martin Luther.

ISBN 0-8254-4028-9　　　　　　　**160 pp.**　　　　　　　**paperback**

Classic Sermons on Family and Home
The erosion of traditional family and biblical values is accelerating at an alarming rate. Dr. Wiersbe has compiled Classic Sermons on Family and Home to help recapture God's enduring truth for the family today.

ISBN 0-8254-4054-8　　　　　　　**160 pp.**　　　　　　　**paperback**

Classic Sermons on the Names of God
Any study of the names of God in Scripture will be enhanced by the classic sermons included in this collection. They feature sermons from Charles H. Spurgeon, G. Campbell Morgan, John Ker, George Morrison, Alexander MacLaren and George Whitefield.

ISBN 0-8254-4052-1　　　　　　　**160 pp.**　　　　　　　**paperback**

Classic Sermons on Overcoming Fear
Classic sermons by such famous preachers as Alexander Maclaren, V. Raymond Edman, Clarence Macartney, George H. Morrison, Charles H. Spurgeon, George W. Truett and others. Wiersbe has chosen sermons which offer insight as well as hope for believers faced with the uncertainty of this pilgrim journey.

ISBN 0-8254-4043-2   **160 pp.**   **paperback**

Classic Sermons on Prayer
Fourteen pulpit giants present the need for and the results of a life permeated with prayer. These sermons by such famous preachers as Dwight L. Moody, G. Campbell Morgan, Charles H. Spurgeon, Reuben A. Torrey, Alexander Whyte, and others, will help you experience the strength and power of God in prayer.

ISBN 0-8254-4029-7   **160 pp.**   **paperback**

Classic Sermons on the Prodigal Son
These sermons by highly acclaimed pulpit masters offer unique insights into perhaps the most famous of Christ's parables. These sermons will provide new understanding of the relationships between the son, father and other son. Believers will also be challenged to apply the wonderful truth of the Father's love to their own lives. .

ISBN 0-8254-4039-4   **160 pp.**   **paperback**

Classic Sermons on the Resurrection of Christ
These sermons represent the best in scholarship, warmed by deep inspiration and enlivened by excitement about what the Resurrection of Christ means to the believer.

ISBN 0-8254-4042-4   **160 pp.**   **paperback**

Classic Sermons on the Second Coming and other Prophetic themes
The second coming of Christ is a promise presented in many New Testament passages. Dr. Wiersbe has marshaled an array of classic sermons on Christ's coming by great preachers such as C. H. Spurgeon, G. Campbell Morgan, C. E. Macartney, Alexander MacLaren, and others.

ISBN 0-8254-4051-3   **160 pp.**   **paperback**

Classic Sermons on Spiritual Warfare
In a timely new compilation of classic sermons, Dr. Warren Wiersbe offers eleven expositions dealing with various facets of Satanic activity. Included are sermons by such outstanding preachers as William Culbertson, Allan Redpath, D. Martyn Lloyd-Jones, G. Campbell Morgan, C. H. Spurgeon, and others.

ISBN 0-8254-4049-1   **160 pp.**   **paperback**

Classic Sermons on Suffering
Sermons by such illustrious preachers as C.H. Spurgeon, Phillips Brooks, John Calvin, Walter A. Maier, George W. Truett, and others that will uplift the depressed, comfort the heartbroken, and be especially useful for the preacher in his pulpit and counseling ministries.

ISBN 0-8254-4027-0   **204 pp.**   **paperback**

Classic Sermons on Worship
In these classic sermons by pulpiteers such as C.H. Spurgeon, John A. Broadus, James S. Stewart, Frederick W. Robertson, G. Campbell Morgan, and Andrew A. Bonar, we discover the true meaning of worship and are challenged to practice it.

ISBN 0-8254-4037-8   **160 pp.**   **paperback**